A DAGGER FOR DANGER

By
Janet Davies
And
Stephen Rayfield

A KATHY CHATSWORTH MYSTERY

Published by:
ESIL Publishing,
638 Buchan Avenue, Oshawa, Ontario L1J 3A3

This book contains an excerpt from the forthcoming book *Pistol Packing Park*. This excerpt has been developed for this edition only and may not reflect the final version in the forthcoming book.

Davies, Janet and Rayfield, Stephen
eBook ISBN: 978-1-7774557-9-8
Softcover ISBN: 978-1-7774557-8-1
Hardcover ISBN: 978-1-9995550-2-3
Audio Book: ISBN: 978-1-7774557-7-4

Dear Reader,

Thank you for downloading our book a Dagger for Danger. We hope you will enjoy the mystery as you join Kathy Chatsworth and Detective Sandy Brampton in tracking down the truth, the lies and the dangers of a family tradition involving a beautiful dagger that has played a part in the betrothal, wounding and killing of women for more than 450 years.

Their investigation into the death of a woman named Shaye grows more bizarre as facts they uncover wrap tendrils around a seemingly unrelated cold case, the murder of a young student named Catrina. What could the brutal stabbing of a 21st century vegan have to do with a twisted tradition from the Middle Ages?

Three people, each with a reason for wanting to see Shaye dead, lead Kathy and Brampton to dig deep into the distant, and not so distant, history of a dangerous dagger.

We hope you enjoy reading this tale. Relax and join in their efforts to solve the puzzle. And, if they survive the convoluted twists of this investigation, we look forward to sharing more collaborations of a nosey journalist and a cautious detective with you in the future.

Janet Davies and Stephen Rayfield

Table of Contents

Chapter 1
About Janet Davies and Stephen Rayfield

1. Emerald Flash

Sunlight flashed across her black-rimmed sunglasses and made Kathy Chatsworth blink, stop walking and look down. The light had bounced off a green stone, half hidden in the vines growing in a tangle under a tall cedar hedge.

She reached down to pick it up and gasped. The stone was attached to a dagger – a long dagger, it looked old, *like something from a film,* she thought, *or an overly ornate thing you find at a costume store.* But this was no toy. It lay heavy in her hand, eight inches from the wicked point to the carved handle where the green stone glinted. Could it be an emerald?

She saw blood on the blade, wet blood, deep red and sticky, with a small, pale green vine leaf trapped on the edge where it had started to congeal.

Kathy's own blood pounded in her ears. *Someone's in trouble,* she thought as a crimson drop fell from the dagger to the ground. She looked about wildly and saw a break in the hedge and a path to a cottage with a beautiful old oak door. The door stood open to a dark hallway. She stopped for a single beat then ran up the path.

Pausing in the hallway she waited for her eyes to catch up, then stepped through a door to the left to a small living room, almost as dim as the hall, with brocade curtains blocking the sun. A figure was curled on the floor. A woman lying on her side, hands clutched at her chest where a deep terrible stain oozed through her fingers, a ragged red flower blooming around them. Kathy ran to her, the bizarre thought springing to her mind *bloodstains are hell to get out of a carpet!* She knelt down, heedless of her own pale blue skirt, and cradled the dying woman in her arms.

The face was ashen, but warm brown eyes fluttered open and stared into Kathy's. Her breath was ragged, her voice no more than a sigh as she stammered "Channel Lane ... Point." Kathy bent closer, cupping the small face, pressing her ear to the bruised lips. "Channel Lane," she whispered again. "His secret ..." The short sentence ended abruptly, no more breaths, no more words, but the eyes stayed open, staring at Kathy, silently pleading.

2. Waiting For Brampton

Kathy held her, rocking slightly. She couldn't think what to do next. Lay the body down? Keep holding it? Shout for help? *Snap out of it!*

Still kneeling, she grabbed a pillow from the couch, placed it on the ruined carpet and tenderly lowered the brunette head. Her eyes filled with tears as the finality of the moment sank in, then she stood up, brushed at her red knees, pulled out her phone and called Sandy.

Detective Sergeant Sandy Brampton and Kathy had known each other for 11 years and she had worked with him on a case or two. They were good friends, had occasionally come close to being more, and they had a mutual appreciation. As the phone rang, she rubbed a palm over her wet eyes thinking *I've made a mess of this. I've touched too much. I should know better.* She felt both relief and trepidation when he picked up.

"Sandy? It's Kathy. I'm okay, but somebody here is not. I'm at 27 Marsh Lane, it's a white cottage behind a cedar hedge. I need you here, and you'd better bring the coroner, but there's no rush. There's a woman, she was alive when I found her but she died in my arms."

Brampton listened patiently, assured her he was on his way and disconnected. *Not a good start,* he thought. *Messy. She knows she's contaminated the scene. I wonder if she has the murder weapon?"*

As he gathered his jacket and keys and walked to his car, he couldn't help thinking *I wonder if she's free for dinner?*

***

Kathy stood silently in the hallway waiting. The dagger lay on a dainty half moon table, painted white with pink cabbage roses. She winced at the red stain beneath the blade and wondered just how much she had contaminated evidence. How could she have known the green stone glinting in the sun was part of a murder weapon?

Her mind wandered to her friendship with Sandy Brampton. He was a homicide detective, she was a journalist – his and her tribes were not famous for having great relationships.

Kathy had enjoyed earning her degree in English Literature but felt aimless in her final year. She thought about teaching. She thought, of course, about writing a novel, but in the end she knew her strengths were research and reporting. Ms. Chatsworth had done stellar work on school newspapers since grade school.

She had an analytic approach to fact gathering and a gift for telling good stories. School newspapers, plus a bit of lucrative ghost writing for lazy but rich kids at school, had honed her natural talents and taught her how to dig and discover, honestly report and imaginatively speculate – and people enjoyed her writing.

The first case she had worked on with Brampton was one she had named *A Death in the Country Inn.* She smiled in the dim hallway, forgetting for a moment the body in the next room. She gave whimsical titles to even the lousiest news stories but her irreverent headlines rarely appeared in print.

It was a murder at a luxury inn and everything pointed to a hapless waiter – motive, evidence and prejudice. But Kathy had uncovered information that exonerated the boy and led to the real killer. Her involvement in the case had been unofficial, so Brampton got the glory – but she got the story.

"Hello Kathy." She jumped as Brampton bent his head and squeezed through the 100-year-old doorway. "You've stumbled on another one," he said, giving her shoulder a quick squeeze. He briefly wondered if that was still acceptable but felt her lean into him before he pushed past to the living room.

"I don't go looking for trouble," she said to his back. "I'll tell you everything I know but it's not much." The woman's last words echoed in her mind, but she would save them until Brampton and the coroner had done their work.

"Do you know who she is?" he asked.

"No. I was on my way to work when I saw something shining in the hedge out there." He was turning slowly to take in every corner of the room. "I picked it up and saw it was some kind of gemstone in the handle of a dagger."

He turned. "A dagger? You mean a knife?" She shook her head and pointed to the half-moon table. "No, I mean a dagger, like in a horror movie or something, and it had blood on it." Her breath caught. "I knew something awful had happened, the blood was wet." She gulped back a sob.

He put his arm around her. "It's okay Kath, you've had a shock. Take a breath. What happened next?"

She pulled air into her lungs and let it out slowly. It wasn't the first time she'd seen a dead body, but it seemed more shocking, somehow obscene, in this pretty little place with roses and brocade and someone bleeding out their life on a peach paisley carpet.

"What happened next? I saw a gap in the hedge, and I came in and found this horrible scene. She was dying Sandy, there was nothing I could do." She took another big breath. "I went to her and held her, I know that was wrong, but it was instinct, and she died in my arms."

He reached for her again but she backed away and went to stand in the sunlight on the flagstone path. He stared after her, then wrote everything she had said in his police notebook.

3. Dr. MacDugon

Dr. Linda MacDugon arrived and knelt by the corpse. The district coroner said nothing, just nodded to Brampton and ignored Kathy. After a few moments she rose.

"Single stab to the chest with that weapon you've got in the evidence bag Sandy," she said. "The bang on her lip is where she fell and hit her face on the coffee table. I'll do some swabbing and sampling to confirm it but that's what it looks like." Dr. MacDugon turned back to the woman lying on the floor and began writing her own notes. Kathy frowned. Would a single blow wreak so much havoc on a woman's breast? She looked again at the dagger in the baggie and shuddered.

"The angle of the blade will help tell if the attacker was taller or shorter," Brampton said and Linda nodded once thinking, *tell me something I don't know.* She turned to Kathy.

"Sorry but we'll need your blouse," she said, not sounding sorry at all. "There's probably blood on your bra, so give me that, too," she strode out of the room, saying over her shoulder, "When I heard it was you, I figured this would happen." She spoke matter-of-factly, but Kathy bristled anyway. "So I came prepared. I haven't got a spare coverall but I've got a T-shirt and sweater you can change into."

Kathy groaned. She liked the blouse she was wearing and feared she might never see it again. The thought of wearing one of MacDugon's t-shirts without a bra did not appeal either. The coroner was annoyingly petite.

The forensics crew arrived and Kathy and Brampton

got out of their way. The doctor returned and handed her a large evidence bag, a small blue t-shirt, and a suspiciously flouncy pink sweater. In the bathroom at the end of the hall, Kathy carefully removed her blouse and bra and stuffed them into the bag, but didn't seal it. Brampton would do that and record the details. She struggled into the T-shirt, tugged it down over her breasts and frowned at her reflection. Adding the cardigan helped a little, but she felt ridiculous and also guilty for caring what she looked like at a time like this. She fingered the frills on the cardigan. She'd never seen Linda MacDugon wear anything like this. She tugged at the frilly edges, trying to make them meet over her bosom, then sighed and stepped back into the hall.

MacDugon nodded to one of her guys to take the evidence bag from Kathy. She was watching the team in their billowing suits and booties meticulously examine the living room. Kathy touched her arm to get her attention. "I'll bring the sweater and t-shirt to the station later today." It would take her 20 minutes to walk home and change, about 19 minutes longer than she wanted to be seen in that get-up. MacDugon gave her a nod and a smile, then waved her away.

As she walked down the stone steps to the path, Kathy thought *what happened here?* And why? Who was the young woman going down her path for the last time, a sad, small bundle on a metal gurney, and what had she been trying to say with her dying words and those pleading eyes?

4. History of The Dagger

Forest of Dean, England, 1560 AD

A cool morning fog spun around his feet as the young woodcutter strode through the forest, looking for a perfect oak log to take back to his father, the carpenter, for a new table. The cry of a grey wolf made the hair on the back of his neck stand up. It was the sound they made when they had a fresh kill.

A hundred yards ahead, the forest floor fell away to his right. The howl came again and he saw at the bottom of the slope a big grey wolf standing over a man who was lying very still. One arm was bent beneath him and appeared broken. A gash in his forehead oozed blood, and the wolf lowered his head to lick at the trickle.

When Jamison saw the figure move, he started down the hill. The wolf spun to face him, growled and bared its sharp teeth. Jamison pulled the axe from his belt, raised it high and hurled it as the wolf leapt. The cold iron embedded itself in the wolf's head and it fell to the ground.

He ran to the creature, knife in hand, and slit its throat. The wolf died instantly and Jamison felt a pang of regret. He looked at the injured man and recognized the face. It was the son of the man who owned these woods, his lord.

Jamison took off his wool jacket and tossed it far from the bloody scene. It was new and precious to him. He tore a sleeve from his linen shirt, easily done as it was old and thin, and used it to bind the head wound. He grasped the rough handle of his axe and pulled, ignoring the sickening sound of blade leaving flesh, then set to work cutting down five small trees and trimming them into poles.

He separated his coarse braided belt into strands to bind the poles to form a litter and used one piece to secure the broken arm to the youth's body. He skinned the wolf and laid its thick pelt on the litter, then laid the young noble on the pelt. The boy groaned and grew paler still.

It was a two-mile walk to the lord's manor house and the litter was heavy, but Jamison, the woodcutter, was strong.

As he neared the house he saw an old man cutting weeds and shouted for help. The old man ran to him, saw what he was dragging and raced to the house. He returned with four strong men to lift the litter onto their shoulders and carry the unconscious lord's son home.

When the gardener heard Jamison's story he touched his shoulder. "You will be rewarded, boy. Go home, now," then he turned and made his way up the half-trimmed path.

Jamison stared at his back, then shrugged and turned wearily back to the forest. What had he expected?

It was late when he arrived home, but he had marked a fine straight oak with his axe and retrieved his wool jacket.

***

Jamison was eating breakfast the next day with his mother and father when a servant from the manor came to their door and asked for him by name. He pushed back his stool on the rough stone floor and went to speak to the man.

"I am Jamison," he said. "I killed the wolf that attacked the lord's son. It attacked me, too," he said defensively. Every animal in the woods belonged to the lord.

The servant just smiled and told the astonished family that Jamison was summoned to the manor for an audience with the lord.

***

The owner of the forest and all the lands around their cottage was sitting in a high carved chair. Beside him sat his son wearing a linen bandage on his head and a velvet sling on his arm. He rose and came to Jamison, unfastening his belt as he came. He held out the fine leather belt.

"Thank you for saving my life. The least I can do is replace your belt. Take this, not a gift but return of a favour."

Jamison had never seen a belt so beautiful, fine leather embossed with roses and vines and finished with a pewter buckle.

The lord stayed seated, but he was smiling. "I thank you for saving my son who is more precious to me than gold. Your father raised you well and also deserves my thanks. I will grant him ownership of the cottage in which you live and of all the lands you can see from your door. You and your descendants shall own this forever, tax-free."

He drew a breath. "You will inherit the land, boy, but for now take this dagger as a token. It was brought from the Holy Land by my great-grandfather. It is a strange weapon, beautiful and powerful. The custom in the land where it was found is for a first-born son to offer a dagger to the woman of his choice. If she accepts it, she accepts the man and they will prick their palms and mingle their blood to seal their troth."

The lord drew from his robe a hammered silver case, hinged and heavy and handed it to the speechless boy

The lord's son clapped Jamison on the back. "We have many such stories in this family, and I'll bet you have stories for me. Our men found the wolf and marveled at your quickness and strength. If you wish to learn more about such things, you must visit me here. My grandfather taught me much about foreign customs." He raised his injured arm and flinched. "And perhaps you can teach me to wield an axe."

5. The Stormont Ritual

Kathy Chatsworth sat back in her chair and exchanged glances with Brampton. It wasn't quite what they had expected to hear from the owner of the murder weapon.

Gordon Stormont finished his story and sat back, too. He was grinning. He had a flair for bringing the past alive. His imagination embellished the solid facts he gathered from family documents, museums and libraries, and he was delighted to take any opportunity to share his sometimes lurid family stories.

It hadn't been hard to trace him. Stormont had reported the dagger missing three days before. Kathy ducked out of an editorial meeting to join Brampton at the Stormont mansion. The place was as ornate as the dagger with too many gables, too many windows and a turret smothered in vines.

They listened quietly as Gordon Stormont told them the history of the dagger, which had been in his family for more than 400 years. It had crossed the Atlantic from England to Canada with his great grandfather after the Great War, one of hundreds of family heirlooms.

"So the knife was used as a token of undying love?" Brampton asked. "That's ironic. Have there been any other unpleasant incidents associated with it?"

Stormont smiled. "Several. About 350 years ago, when Anderson Stormont was laughed at by the lady he wished to marry, he flew into a rage and stabbed her in the heart. No one else was present, and Anderson insisted it was self-defense," he coughed delicately. "She was, by all accounts, a spirited lady and Anderson went unpunished."

Kathy was aghast. "Seriously? He stabbed her?" Brampton patted her hand, but she snatched it away.

Stormont continued. "In 1825, Gregory Stormont accidentally hit his beloved's wrist instead of her palm. There were others present on that occasion, and they all agreed he was nervous and probably drunk. They rushed her to a doctor, she was stitched up and survived, but it left a nasty scar. In her portrait she is wearing gloves. Did you see it as you came in? It's in the hall, painted by William Matthew Prior. An ugly portrait, too much like folk art for my taste."

"I'll look out for it as we leave," Brampton said drily. "Carry on please."

Stormont smiled agreeably. "Of course, where was I? Ah yes, Amanda Stormont and her scar. All stitched up, she accepted his proposal, they married and she bore him four sons. She liked to remind him of how he'd botched the ceremony, never pricked her or mingled their blood. I suppose she was suggesting they'd never really sealed the deal." He rubbed his hands together with glee. He loved family stories. "Family letters tell how she would playfully threaten him with a knife at dinner, but they had a long, happy marriage. Fifty-five years, I believe."

Kathy snorted with amusement. "So when did the deerskin gloves become part of the ritual?"

Stormont answered readily, "As far as we can tell it was after Anderson Stormont killed his bride-to-be. He grew rather melancholy," said Stormont and Kathy rolled her eyes. "When he was ready to try another proposal, he stuck with tradition but was understandably cautious about wielding the knife. Three years after the death of his first intended, he proposed to a young heiress who knew nothing about her predecessor. He had the deer-skin gloves made so he wouldn't have to actually touch the dagger and introduced them into the ceremony. Anderson wore the gloves and removed the left one just long enough to scratch his palm and hers. There's a faint bloodstain inside one glove."

Stormont steepled his fingers. "He married the unsuspecting girl, largely ignored her and was thrown from a horse 20 years later and died."

Good, thought Kathy. "Any more incidents? Or did the world grow less tolerant of family ritual as a defense for murder?" Brampton threw her a warning glance, but Stormont was unfazed.

"No more incidents that we know of," he confirmed, but Kathy wasn't finished.

"So the Stormont men have been doing this," she stopped short of saying *bullshit,* "this ceremony ever since?"

He beamed. "My great grandfather did the ceremony when he proposed to my great grandmother, and she found it quite romantic. She used to show me the tiny scar on her palm. She was rather proud of it."

6. Disappearance of The Dagger

"Right," Brampton said briskly. "Thanks for the background. Fascinating stuff. How did the dagger go missing?"

Stormont's smile faded. "It's kept in its box, a very old box made of oak."

"What happened to the silver sheath?" Kathy interrupted, and Stormont cocked an eyebrow.   "Sheath? Oh, the one from the lord, yes. I never saw it. If I remember the story right, my great grandfather had it melted down in 1915 to go to the war effort. I suppose the gemstone would have been worth a pretty penny, but the family never considered parting with the dagger. They just wrapped it in velvet and kept it in an old oak box after that."

He gave a little laugh. "We don't make a big thing of it, the ceremony, the proposal and pricking of palms. It sounds daft, but with so many traditions biting the dust these days, we like to keep that one going. There's no harm in it."

Kathy felt her jaw tighten and slid a side eye to Brampton who ignored her. "When did it actually disappear?" he asked.

Gordon frowned. "Must have been at the charity function. The house was full of strangers last Friday, about 200 of them milling about the house and gardens. Any one of them could have taken it."

"You mean it was kept out in the open? You don't lock it up?" Kathy asked in surprise.

He looked uncomfortable. "The box doesn't lock. The key was lost years ago, and it's just an old thing, after all, it means nothing to anybody else. We keep it on the sideboard with other family things, treasures and tat together. It's never been a problem before."

They were now faced with 200 suspects. Brampton was going to need help.

"Does anyone else know the whole history of the dagger?" Kathy asked.

"Dr. Kenneth Rivers at the University teaches history of the Middle Ages and he's studied Stormont history for years. I can email him to introduce you if you like."

Good to his word, he composed the email there and then, copying them both, and Kathy was pleasantly surprised when minutes later Dr. Rivers replied. He would be glad to talk with them and was sure he could help, as he was one of the foremost Canadian experts on the Middle Ages, etc.   Brampton skipped the two paragraphs setting out Rivers' qualifications and looked to the bottom to see if he had suggested a date. He had not.

They were invited to make an appointment via the On-line Student Calendar. He rolled his eyes and glanced sideways at Kathy to see her in mid-eyeroll, too.

They stepped from the dark hallway into bright sunshine and Brampton snapped his fingers. "Dammit! I forgot to look at the portrait." She smacked his arm, pulled out her phone to check the time, then gave him a quick hug and headed for the street. He watched her walk away. *Double damn. I should have asked her out to dinner.*

Kathy was wondering as she walked, *Why would the Stormont family honour such a stupid tradition?* And what could it possibly have to do with Shaye Alderson? They had discovered the victim was a staff writer at Hilton's Bazaar Magazine, just 26 years old. Why would anyone want to kill her? Could it really have something to do with the Stormonts?

7. Cold Case Coincidence

In her spare time Kathy took an interest in cold murder cases. As she prepared to start profiles on people connected with Shaye Alderson's murder, she thought back to another knife murder that had happened seven years ago. A college student on March break was found naked in a rented lakeside cottage, stabbed in the heart.

Police concluded she had walked out of the shower and surprised a burglar. No sign of a struggle, no bruises on her arms or hands, and just one stab wound to the heart. Perhaps the burglar stabbed her in a panic. Perhaps he was high. The really strange thing was the body had been washed and placed carefully on the bed and covered with a duvet. Her hair spread out on the pillow. It seemed like a lot of care for a burglar to lavish on someone they had killed in a panic. And the weapon had never been found.

Could it have been a dagger? she wondered. Was the student somehow connected to the Stormont family? She made a note to pull information on that old case.

8. Suspect Deborah Citlali

Kathy rested her chin on her hand as she studied the new profile sheet. Whenever she looked into a murder, she put together a profile sheet on every suspect. She was currently looking at Deborah Citlali, a co-worker of Shaye's at the magazine that was part of Wade Williams publishing empire. They were colleagues, but not exactly friends. Deborah had been heard to say she would kill to have Shaye's job.

She was a society columnist, but impatient to do more. Writing about fancy parties, weddings and fundraisers was not real journalism, she felt, more like pandering to the rich. What she longed for were grittier stories, true-crimes and victims. Real investigations she could sink her teeth into.

Kathy had talked to people at the magazine, and most seemed to find her cold, calculating, not a team player. She was political, flirted with senior people, but pretty much ignored her peers, unless she wanted something from them.

Deborah had been passed over for a promotion that was given to Shaye Alderson. She had been with the company longer, but this newcomer, who'd come from a lowly position as copywriter at the ad agency, got the plum promotion. She was angry.

Even more interesting, Ms. Citlali had recently written about the Stormont family and touched on the dagger and the peculiar pre-nuptial ceremony.

She had an interest in knives in general and the Stormont dagger in particular. She'd wheedled permission from the family to take it to a blacksmith to be cleaned and sharpened. The Stormonts regarded the dagger as a bit of a joke, but Deb treated it with respect, she wanted to care for it and preserve it. She had shown it to her martial arts mentor who had been suitably impressed and, later, discovered Deborah alone in a practice room doing elaborate fight moves with the dagger, culminating in her sinking it up to the hilt in a practice dummy's heart.

Kathy shuddered. It was one thing to see knife attacks in the movies, but now she had seen what a real knife does to a real body, and it wasn't pretty.

She stood up and refreshed her tea before reading about an incident at Wade Williams Christmas party. Nobody knew how it started, but everyone saw how it finished. A heated discussion between the two women ended with Shaye slapping Deborah's face. That was shocking enough, but the response was jaw-dropping. Deborah rotated on her heel and threw a vicious high kick at Shaye's head. She pulled it at the last moment, just hitting her shoulder and knocking her to the ground.

Witnesses said she was bouncing on the balls of her feet looking menacing and slightly ridiculous before she calmed down and helped Shaye to her feet.

As a registered martial arts fighter Deb was under rule of law to use her skills only for defense. If she'd really hurt Shaye she'd have been in big trouble. But despite the dramatics, Shaye had shrugged it off and everyone just put it down to the rum punch.

Kathy was now very interested. A bad relationship with the victim, an expert with knives, an interest in the

Stormont dagger and she had been seen actually using it. It felt almost too easy.

After running it past Brampton, Kathy decided to take action. She would join the mixed martial arts club where Deb worked out, talk her way into being partnered with her and observe this prime suspect at close quarters. *But not too close,* she thought as she closed the file.

9. Good With A Knife

Tiger Breth Martial Arts Club met on Tuesdays. Kathy wondered if the spelling was deliberate or if the sign painter gave them a break on cost to avoid having to re-paint it.

She discussed buddying up with Deb when she signed up. "I want some exercise," she told Curtis Manga, the owner, "and I want to learn how to defend myself."

"With a knife?" he asked doubtfully.

"I don't like guns," she trilled. "They scare me. Anyway, I'm more likely to have a knife handy if somebody breaks in and I'm in the kitchen, right?" Manga did a *whatever* shrug and swiped her platinum card.

"I don't get you girls," he said as he handed it back. "But if you want to work with knives, Deb's your man."

"You have a woman knife fighter? That's interesting. Should I bring my own knife?"

He sighed. "Please don't. We got everything you need. I'll tell Deb."

Feeling over-dressed in her new blue tracksuit, she turned up at six sharp to find Deborah Citlali waiting. She expected a cool reception, but the woman smiled and shook her hand. "You like knives, eh? Cool. Come on," and she led the way into the gym.

...

As they worked through exercises and drills, Deb commented constantly on Kathy's movements in a clear and helpful way. Where was the stuck-up, resentful, violent woman she'd heard about? After an hour Kathy was disheveled, sweaty and dizzy while Deb was still bouncing on the balls of her feet.

"Listen up guys," Manga called as he unwrapped strips of cloth from his hands. "Deb's got a tournament on the weekend. Can some of you stay while she practices with me? She wants to get the feel of working in front of a crowd."

Deb turned to Kathy. "Will you stay? I'd like to hear your thoughts on the artistic side of my performance." Kathy looked surprised and a little worried. Deborah frowned. "Don't worry," she said tartly. "I don't expect you to say anything very helpful, but it's not just about combat, the judges look at style, too. It's an art form." Kathy raised her eyebrows. "Just tell me how it looks. I'm going for fluid and seamless and graceful, I guess." She jerked her head towards the young men jostling each other and laughing at some joke. "These morons don't get that, so maybe you can help me out here."

Kathy nodded. "I'll try. I'm not sure how much I can help since I've got like two hours experience."

"Hey, at least you know what it feels like now. You'll see the overall action more than the fine points which is helpful, too." Deb punched her arm and sprinted off to the mat. *Ouch!* Kathy rubbed her arm and took a ringside position.

10. In The Shower With Deb

Manga and Deborah took to the mat and performed the ceremonial greeting, then things got physical fast. Kathy flinched as she watched twists and thrusts, dodges and slashes.

Deb was good. Several times she broke through the instructor's defenses to hold her knife at his padded neck or press the point to his thick chest protector.

Kathy couldn't follow all the moves but it was obvious Deb had more than attack skills. She could psyche out her opponent, moving in ways that made her look vulnerable but had the effect of wrong-footing her attacker.

Each time, just before making 'the kill' she yelled out something that sounded like, "Eeyass!"

After the session, Manga patted Deb on the back and headed for the locker room. Deb called out to the other observers, "Thanks guys, I'm beat but maybe see you in Shonseys later." To Kathy she said, "Talk to me while we shower."

Kathy was aghast. "I prefer to shower at home, But I'll come in with you."

In the tiny locker room she perched on a stool as Deb showered not 12 inches away behind a pineapple patterned curtain. "So what do you think?" Deborah called cheerfully.

You can do this, Kathy told herself. "I did see one thing," she began. There was silence behind the curtain. "It was amazing, the first time you broke through his defense and got your knife to his throat, you did a double twirl before you lunged."

"Thanks," shouted Deborah over the running water.

"But it looked kind of over the top," said Kathy. Silence. "It just looked showy," Kathy soldiered on. "Maybe a waste of energy? Like a single twirl would have done?" She had no idea what she was talking about and held her breath.

Deborah peered round the pineapple curtain. "You're right," she said. "Double twirl was showmanship. It could have opened me up for attack." She ducked back into the shower and shouted, "Anything else?"

Feeling more confident, Kathy told her everything she'd noticed, truthfully not much, but she embellished it with phrases she'd picked up in prepping for going undercover.

Deborah listened intently as she toweled her naked body, quite unaware of Kathy's discomfort in the confined space.

At home with a glass of wine, steeping in a hot bath to ease her muscles Kathy reflected. This was not the woman the magazine staff had described, difficult, aggressive, unhappy. She seemed completely engaged in her sport, generous with her expertise and genuinely interested in Kathy's thoughts.

She thought of what Deborah had said as they walked to their cars. With her hair still wet and eyes aglow, doing that funny bouncing walk, she'd said, "Fighting with a knife is a noble art. It's got a bad rap, but in its pure form it's amazing. Fear surrounds you, but at the moment you stab them," she paused and laughed, squeezing Kathy's shoulder. "I mean, when you strike, when you win, you feel like a god. The Winner! The Taker. A real kill it must feel like absorbing their life energy, it must feel amazing." Then she made a 'toodles' wave with both hands, got in her car and drove away, leaving Kathy feeling slightly sick.

Now, lying in her bath, she pressed a finger hard into her breastbone and held it there, thinking about a practice dummy leaking sawdust, and then about a woman leaking blood into a paisley carpet.

11. What's In A Name

Next morning, nibbling on toast, Kathy glanced over her cold case notes on the student who had walked out of the shower and into a knife. She'd made a note to follow up on the missing weapon, now she added a note to probe for any connection between Deborah and the murdered student.

Later that day, sitting in a tedious planning meeting at work, her thoughts drifted. The cold case victim had been called Catrina Somers. She doodled the name Catrina in curly cursive writing. Beside it she wrote Shaye, the name of the woman who had died in her arms. As the head of her department droned on, she tapped her pen on the pad and wrote both names in block capitals – then felt a cold trickle in her stomach.

Kathy could read upside down, sideways and backwards. It's handy for reading documents on other people's desks. Now she read that last name backwards, EYAHS. It was a nonsense word but it would sound like *Eyass* if you said it out loud – and Kathy had heard it said very loud indeed, every time Deb Citlali struck a killing blow in her make believe knife fight.

12. Clever Margaret

People think investigative journalism is all excitement and discoveries. In reality it's gathering notes, verifying sources, checking and rechecking information and following leads that too often run into dead ends. Like detecting, there's a lot of footwork but these days it's not hard on the shoe leather. You can learn a lot from the Internet.

Births, deaths, marriages, divorces, vehicle registration, building permits, graduation records, it's all there, along with surprising amounts of personal data from club memberships to friendships gone bad.

Kathy Chatsworth was adept at mining online records. All you need is a starting point, a name, a date, an event, maybe a quote. She had the words of a dying woman. "Channel Lane ... point."

She was on her way to visit the company library and the historian who worked in the archives. Margaret Hooper was a fountain of knowledge and an insatiable reader who devoured fiction, blogs, biographies, true crime, epic fantasies, historical romance, political memoirs, you name it. Even more interesting, she remembered pretty much everything she read. This ability, together with the round tortoiseshell glasses she wore on her head, around her neck, dangling from her mouth and, occasionally, on her face, earned her the affectionate nickname Google.

Margaret glanced up over the top of her glasses, and beamed. "How can I help you, Kath?" She turned her eyes back to the screen but gestured for Kathy to sit.

"The recent murder victim," said Kathy. "The one that died in my arms." Margaret looked up sympathetically and gave an encouraging nod.

"Before she died, she whispered Channel Lane, Point, Channel Lane. Do you have any idea what or where that is?"

Margaret sat back and drummed her fingers on the old oak desk, then smiled. "It rings a bell. There was a murder about seven years ago. A student. Let me look it up. Do you need it now or can I get back to you?"

Kathy's mind raced. "Any top line information you can give me would be great and let me have details later if you find them."

The older woman struggled up from the oversized velvet armchair she favoured over modern office chairs. She made it to her feet on the second try, straightened her back with a click and motioned Kathy to follow. Down the hall, past two offices, she opened the door to a large file room, scanned labels on cabinets before choosing one and opened and closed drawers noisily until she found what she was after. She thumped a fat brown folder on the table and lowered herself carefully onto the flimsy, hard backed file room chair.

"Here it is. The victim's name is," she looked up apologetically over her glasses, "I mean *was* Catrina Somers, home from University and staying in a rental cottage out at Channel Lane Point. Stabbed as she came out of the shower. Interrupted a burglar, police think, stabbed once in the heart. Died almost instantly."

Kathy's eyes grew wide, Margaret noticed. "That

means something to you, eh? Dr. MacDugon did the autopsy." She flipped the page. "Catrina was at McGill taking a business course, with a minor in ancient history. Good grades." Kathy shifted impatiently. "Hmm, let's see, guy named Rivers was her history professor, blah blah, she had just handed in a group project to him." She flipped the file shut. "Dr. Mac can tell you about the corpse, but maybe the professor, or the kids who worked on that project with her can tell you about the live girl."

Kathy felt a chill. Brampton did not believe in coincidence, and neither did she. Shaye's dying words were the address of Catrina's murder. If she knew why the student had died, she might learn why another young woman died in her arms seven years later. Dr. Rivers, self-proclaimed expert on the dagger and Catrina's teacher was a good place to start.

13. Call Me Ken

She called the university and was told the professor was too busy to be disturbed but was available afternoons for student visits. She used the University Student online booking app to make an appointment for 2:00 p.m. and thought how things had changed since she left school.

Grabbing lunch in a nearby café, she made notes, caught up on messages and pondered whether to let Brampton know what she was up to.   She hadn't shared her thoughts on the connections between the two murders and he would probably scold her for that. She grinned at the word, then blushed and shook her head.

She tossed her sandwich wrapper in the bin, pushed past two students in the doorway, locked in an embrace, and wondered if Brampton would *ever* ask her out.

At 2 o'clock sharp Dr. Rivers met her at his office door.

"Ms. Chatsworth, how nice to see you. I do hope I can be of help, what's on your mind?"

"Dr. Rivers, I'm tracking down a cold case from seven years ago, Catrina Somers was killed out at Channel Lane Point. I understand she was your student?"

Shock flashed on Rivers' face, but he recovered, smiled and moved aside, gesturing for Kathy to step in.

"Call me Ken," he said warmly. "Dr. Rivers sounds so formal." He sat down behind the desk, straightened a pen and a picture, sat back and crossed his legs and leveled his gaze at her.

"Catrina was in my ancient history class, a clever girl and very conscientious. She had just handed in a group assignment when," he shuddered. "When it happened. So tragic what happened to her." He sighed. "They never found the killer. The police don't think it was anyone she knew. A robbery, they said, she surprised some thug who attacked her. Tragic."

Kathy murmured agreement, noting his neat summation of what had probably happened. She let a beat go by. Where should she go next? Find out the others in Catrina's study group.

"Dr. Rivers, um Ken, if it's not confidential can you give me the names of the people in her project group?"

Rivers looked relieved and reached for his laptop. "No problem, that's public information, let me pull up the old class list."

The Apple notebook lit up as he touched the keys and began to scroll through files.

"Here we are. There were four, Catrina, Everett Jones, Tabatha Everson, and Grant Ashbury the lone male. They were a serious bunch, I didn't know them well and, of course, I know even less about them now," he sighed and closed the computer. "Some students stay in touch, but most move on, get busy with careers and life and never think of their old professors." She opened her mouth to say something nice, but stopped. What did she know about old professors? She had avoided most of hers like the plague. She thanked him, shook hands and left.

14. Catrina's Classmates

Back in her own office she trawled the Internet for Catrina's old classmates. Through LinkedIn she discovered Everett Jones was now Mrs. Mayfair and lived in Vancouver, British Columbia. Despite having two children in six years, she had risen to the position of creative director of a small ad agency. Kathy immediately ruled her out as a suspect. With a demanding job and two small kids *she'd barely have time to do her nails, let alone murder someone on the other side of the country,* Kathy thought.

Next was Tabatha Everson. Her LinkedIn account showed she was regional sales manager in Québec for a pharmaceutical company. Interesting. Had Catrina or Shaye been drugged? *Keep it simple,* she thought. Catrina was in the shower. Still, she jotted a reminder to see the autopsy report, took a swig of cold coffee and continued.

Last was Grant Ashbury. Her eyebrows rose when she instantly got four hits on the name. Grant was head of computer technology for a publishing empire. The back of her neck tingled when she saw it included Hilton's Bazaar, the magazine where Shaye Alderson had worked. Another coincidence? She drew a thick black circle around his name and decided she would definitely go to meet this man, but first she'd find out from the professor how the team members had got along.

****

"Dr. Rivers, Ken, it's Kathy Chatsworth," she said into the phone, "I have a couple of questions about Catrina Somers's project group. Is this a good time?"

He didn't answer immediately, but when he did his voice was full of bonhomie. "Yes, yes, of course. I'm grading papers and I'll take any excuse for a break. What do you need to know?"

"How did the three girls get along? Were they friends? Was there friction? Do you know how they worked together?"

She could picture him rearranging pens before answering. "It was an interesting group," he said after a pause. "The three ladies," she winced at the word, "were all very dynamic, very bright. I believe they worked together well. Everett Jones was the natural leader, but they were one of the more cohesive groups that year."

Kathy made notes. "What about Grant? Was he okay with Everett taking the lead?"

A small sigh. "Ah yes, Grant, nice boy, very enthusiastic. He got quite excited about archaeological artifacts, loved history. He worked well with the girls and, truth be told, he had a crush on Catrina. He didn't hide it very well. She didn't complain, but I could tell from their emails, which were copied to me, she kept him at arms length. It was amusing to read between the lines."

So Grant Ashbury had been sweet on Catrina. He must have been distraught when she was killed. Meeting Mr. Ashbury would be her next step.

15. Suspect Grant Ashbury

As Kathy drove to Ashbury's office, she wondered again if she should update Sandy. When she worked with him she was usually content to play the role of reporter researching for an article, but she didn't hesitate to use her police connections if she thought it would help in an interview. Brampton didn't object to her methods, as long as she was careful. What he did *not* like was being kept out of the loop.

She drummed a nervous beat on the wheel, weighing up how annoyed he might be. She told herself she didn't know enough about Grant Ashbury to bother him with it. She would give him a call as soon as she'd finished her interview. If he wanted to scold her, she could take it. She blushed again and flipped on the radio.

***

The reception area of Ward Williams Publishing was huge. White leather couches floated on an improbably turquoise floor and a water feature splashed cheerfully down the wall behind the receptionist. Kathy wondered how often the young woman felt the urge to visit the loo in a day.

The receptionist greeted her and offered a visitors book to sign. "Do you have an appointment with Mr. Ashbury?" she asked. Kathy answered carefully, not wanting to give away too much.

"Actually, I just have a few questions for an article I'm working on," she said, leaning in conspiratorially. The receptionist blinked and glanced down at the book. "Oh Ms.

Chatsworth, how nice to meet you! I'm a big fan of your writing. I'm sure it will be fine. Grant, I mean Mr. Ashbury, is a great guy. I'm sure he'll be glad to help." She shoved the book to one side and hit the security button, nodding to an elderly security guard who stood at the glass doors. He stepped aside as they slid open.

Kathy straightened her jacket and walked through. *First hurdle passed.* Grant Ashbury was not in his corner office, and she faltered, looking left and right. A woman who had been standing in the hallway stabbing at her phone leaned in. "Can I help? Grant's out on the floor I believe, but he should be back in a few minutes."

Kathy took the moment to introduce herself, thinking she might learn something about Ashbury while she waited.

"Hi, I'm Kathy Chatsworth, I'm writing an article about the death of Shaye Alderson. Have you worked here long? Did you know her?"

The woman looked pleased. "Me? I've been here about three years. It's an interesting place, a lot of fun." She let the smile fade. "Oh, yes, Shaye, I knew her. Great girl. Always took time to ask how you're doing, and actually listened when you told her. We spend so much time online you forget how nice it is to talk to someone in person."

Kathy nodded and before the other woman could expand on her theme, she broke in. "I've met Grant socially, but I don't really know him. Can you tell me a little more about him before we sit down to talk?"

The woman glanced over her shoulder as if to check no one was listening, but her answer was innocuous. "Grant really *is* a nice guy. He's head of IT here and really helpful. He runs a small group, but everybody likes to have Grant, and because I'm right next door he always does quick fixes for me. He's one of those positive types you know? Says things like, 'There are no problems, only opportunities," she frowned, "or is it challenges? I don't remember, but he's always up and cheerful. Always there, and always up."

Kathy thought he sounded exhausting. "Did Grant know Shaye?"

The woman glanced over her shoulder again, this time more dramatically. "Not to tell tales out of school, Grant was *sweet* on Shaye. I believe they had some history, and he was really upset when she was murdered." She thought about it and added, "We all were, of course, but Grant took it really hard."

They had history, that was interesting. Before she could ask more, a tap on the shoulder made her jump. Grant Ashbury had come up behind and stood smiling at her.

16. The Man And The Mask

"Well, hello Kathy Chatsworth," he said with a little bow. "I remember you from the Heart Gala. What brings you here?"

She held out her hand and he shook it. "I was hoping you had a few minutes to talk. I'm pulling together information on Shaye Alderson, and wondered if you could tell me something about her as a person."

Ashbury's smile faded. "Absolutely. Are you working with the police?"

"No," she said, a little too quickly. "Right now I'm gathering information for an article." Sandy would be upset if she mentioned the investigation, particularly since he didn't know she was there.

"Come into my office."

Kathy took a luxurious leather chair by the window, Grant sat opposite and said, "How can I help?"

"I don't know much about Shaye and I'm trying to build a picture. Did you know her well?"

His expression was blank, almost as if he hadn't heard the question. Kathy waited. Would he be candid? Was he putting up a mask?

He smiled. "I'm VP of computer technology, and I want all our people to feel comfortable with our systems. When someone new starts, I sit with them and explain the technology available."   He stopped and waited for the next question.

"You've got a lot of people here. I met two today and they both said how easy you are to work with." He made a dismissive gesture and she pressed on. "But what about Shaye. Did you have much to do with her?"

He sat back and unbuttoned his jacket. "Actually, we knew each other before she joined Wade Williams, so, yes, I knew her a little better than others here."

"Can I ask how you knew her before?" Kathy jotted a note on her pad before smiling up at him. "If you're not comfortable answering that's fine, I don't want to pry."

Ashbury glanced over to his desk. Kathy followed his gaze and was startled to see his screensaver was a picture of a smiling Shaye.

**

"We were at high school together," he said. "We were in the drama club and in graduation year we were in a play together, not the lead roles," he laughed, "just support characters, but we had some interesting dialogue together."

Kathy could see him remembering. The neutral mask slipped and was replaced with a faraway look, as if a warm breeze had touched him.

"We had a couple of dates but nothing too serious. We were going off in the summer to work and then going to different universities in the Fall. Shaye didn't think it would work to have a long-distance relationship," he said it in a mocking, sing-song voice. "I agreed, of course." He brushed at something invisible on his trousers. "Maybe if we'd gone to the same university the romance would have carried on." Kathy heard longing in his voice and did not interrupt.

He picked up a pen and flipped it back and forth, then cut his eyes back. "When she came to work here, I hoped to rekindle our relationship. We talked outside of work, met for coffee sometimes, but she made it clear she thought of me as a big brother rather than boyfriend material."

"Did that affect your relationship at work? Did you feel awkward? Was there any ill feeling?"

"Oh no," he seemed surprised by the suggestion. "God no. I'd never make things awkward for Shaye. We got along fine, and who knows," he said almost defiantly, "we might have grown close again given time – if she'd lived."

Kathy looked down at her list of questions. She hadn't anticipated this kind of openness or his obvious love for the girl. He was voluntarily making himself a person of interest. She had to learn more.

"Thanks for your candor, and that's enough about Shaye, for now. What about you? I'd like to know a little more about Grant Ashbury."

She was not surprised to see the mask slip back into place.

"I grew up in this town and lived here all my life," he said, flipping his $200 Cross pen back and forth. "I took computer science at the University of Toronto and Chris Wade, son of the founder of this company, was my roommate. He was taking business studies so he could eventually run the family business. We took holidays together, I met his family, we got along. I graduated with excellent grades and they offered me a job." He finished and raised an eyebrow as if to say *your turn.*

"Wow, that's interesting. What about outside work? What do you do when you're not slaving in front of a computer screen?"

"I'm not married," he smiled, "not yet. No dogs or cats. I work long hours. One thing I do still enjoy is history, the Middle Ages to be precise. It was my minor in university." He tossed the pen and it landed on the glass table with a clatter. "I know about the dagger."

17. Grant Remembers

Kathy jumped. "What dagger?"

He gave her a knowing look. "The Stormonts are related to the Wades, so I've actually seen the famous Stormont dagger and I've always been interested in history. It's an odd combination, computer science and the Middle Ages, but you know a lot of science fiction borrows heavily from traditions and stories of that era. There's nothing new under the sun, and we can learn a lot from studying how things were done in the past."

Kathy was fascinated to see the corporate mask slip again as he spoke about personal interests. Should she return to Shaye? He had chosen to mention the dagger.

"It must be hard for you," she said carefully. "Having feelings for Shaye and then losing her to," she stopped, lost for words. "I mean, having a kind of connection to the ..."

He gave a little snort. "A connection to the instrument of her destruction?" He looked over to his computer screen, then back to Kathy. No mask, just an open face and a level gaze.

"I know a lot about the dagger that killed her," he said simply. "It's the only positive thing about the tragedy. If she had to die, at least it was a noble death. The dagger is part of history, and now so is she. She's part of its history, one of a long line of memorable women to whom the dagger brought happiness or pain."

It was an odd comment and Kathy filed it away to

think about later. She finished her list of prepared questions, he answered them easily and she found herself agreeing with his colleagues. Grant Ashbury was a nice guy. A little nerdy perhaps, carrying a torch for a girl who had no interest in him and harboring strange ideas about magical daggers, but a nice guy.

"One more thing. How well did you know Catrina Somers? I know you were at school together, I've talked with Dr. Rivers about the group project."

At the mention of her name his eyes flashed, before he could lower them. He picked up the pen again but she saw the tightening of the jaw, a narrowing of the eyes. When he looked up, the expressionless mask was in place. *Is this just something he does when he was thinking?* Kathy wondered. To navigate company politics, he might have learned to hide his true thoughts and emotions.

"Catrina Somers, wow, I haven't heard that name for a long time. Yes, I was part of that group, and as I recall it turned into a big mess. Catrina was supposed to hand in our paper, but the professor claimed she hadn't. It was our final paper copy and none of us had the complete version, there wasn't a backup."

He frowned, remembering. Kathy waited. "After Catrina died, Everett, the group leader, checked in with Rivers to make sure he'd received our paper." He gave another little snort. "Everett was the type to think of that even after a friend was murdered, and she was the right one to do it because Rivers was more lenient with the girls, more agreeable. He wore his hair just a little too long, even had highlights put in, which cracked the guys up."

Kathy shifted impatiently. *Just get on with it.*

"He told Everett Catrina hadn't turned in the paper, so

we had to really hustle and write up another final version using our notes. We put our bits and pieces together. We knew it wouldn't be as polished, but we did our best, and then the bastard was going to ding us for late marks, which would have been incredibly unfair." He was sounding like an indignant young student.

"We went as a group to argue that Catrina was about to hand it in when she was killed, it wasn't our fault it was late, so why should we be punished?" He stopped suddenly and looked sheepish. "Rivers agreed and gave us back the late marks he'd deducted, so everything was okay, I mean, it was fair."

He must have known he sounded insensitive, but he held her gaze and Kathy was the first to look away. She left shortly after, Ashbury inviting her to call any time.

Back in her car she mulled things over. There was no evidence the murdered women had known each other, but they had two things in common, Channel Lane Point and Grant Ashbury.

18. Debrief At Breakfast

Brampton was feeling good as he drove to Rosy's Diner to meet Kathy. It was their routine to meet for breakfast and compare notes, and he looked forward to it. Kathy brought new insights and perspective to the facts. He often thought she'd make a good cop if she could stand the discipline. He smiled as he turned into the parking lot. Today he had information that would blow her socks off.

"Howdy," he called to Lucy the morning waitress as he slid into their regular booth by the wall. They never sat at the window, too many distractions, too many people they knew walking by.

The diner hadn't changed much in all the time he'd been eating there. He doubted it had changed much since it opened in 1949. The tables were black and white flecked Formica but he remembered when they were battered old wood, burnished by decades of diners' elbows. He missed the scars and the wobbly hearts, the I Love You's and phone numbers carved into them. Five years ago, Rosy had them refinished. The retro Formica was a nod to their past, but all those sweet emotions were invisible now, hidden beneath the plastic.

Kathy arrived dressed business stylish as always. She slipped out of her jacket before shimmying across the bench seat opposite him. She smiled and squeezed his hand briefly. It was always briefly.

"You doing, okay?"

"Couldn't be better."

As Lucy approached to take their orders, she wondered, not for the first time, just what was their relationship. Sometimes they were relaxed and smiling, sometimes deadly serious. She wouldn't see them for months at a time, and then they'd come in regularly, sometimes twice a week, and have breakfast together, deep in discussion. She was sure they were more than business friends, but she rarely saw them touch, let alone hug or kiss.

"Scrambled eggs, bacon, fried tomatoes and brown toast for me please," he said briskly and smacked the menu down.

"I'll have an egg white omelet with mushrooms, brown toast and tea, if you please," said Kathy without looking at the menu. Lucy jotted down the orders, smiled and stole a glance at Kathy's left hand ring finger before walking away.

"So how are you really doing?" he asked.

"I'm *fine*," she said, emphasizing the last word and doing a little jazz hands.

"Really?" he pressed. "It's only a couple of days since a woman died in your lap. That'll leave a bruise on anyone, so, I'll ask again, how are you really doing?"

Kathy relented, reached across and touched his hand again. Lucy had her back turned and missed it. "All things considered, I'm doing okay," she said. "I sometimes think if I'd stopped there sooner maybe I could have prevented it, but then I realize I wouldn't have stopped because I wouldn't have seen the jewel in the bushes. I wouldn't have noticed the open door. I don't think I could have helped in any way," her voice broke. "I suppose maybe it was meant to be."

Images from that day passed through her mind. She

blinked to stop the parade and brought her eyes back to Brampton.

Concern was etched on his face and he fought the urge to take her hands in his. Instead, he smiled and shrugged.

"How did your meeting with Grant Ashbury go?"

19. Nice Guy Grant

She smiled and was glad she had told him about her visit after the fact. He'd taken it well. No scolding. "Learn anything good?" He leaned back to let Lucy place his loaded breakfast down and refill his coffee.

Kathy closed her eyes and inhaled the aroma of bacon before answering. "Well the first thing I learned was I wouldn't want to play poker with him. He's got this ability to go corporate and put up a mask. But when he talks about personal things, I saw the mask slip several times."

Brampton paused with a piece of toast halfway to his mouth. "Personal things? Like what? Things that make him a potential suspect?"

"Well," she said shaking out her napkin, raising her fork and looking glumly at the flaccid egg white omelet. "One thing is he dated Shaye Alderson back in high school."

"What? Like casual? Heavy? What kind of dating?"

"They were in a play together, but they were just support characters," Kathy replied and ignored his bewildered look. "He was attracted to her, I think he was quite the nerd, excellent grades in math and stuff, but unlikely to have other opportunities to get so close to a babe. Maybe he took their acting roles too seriously, and his hormones kicked in and he asked her out."

She paused and chewed, thinking how to sum up her impressions. "It sounded one-sided, like he read far more into it than was there. They had a couple of dates, but she said because they were going to different universities a long-distance relationship would be too hard, so she didn't want to get too involved. She was probably being kind, letting him down easy, using it as an excuse to not be his girl." Brampton frowned, remembering a similar conversation with a girl in high school.

"He's a smart guy, but still a bit nerdy and needy," she said. "I was surprised he opened up like that. I didn't expect him to come across as vulnerable."

Brampton nodded, gestured for her to continue and renewed his attack on the enjoyable bacon and eggs.

"When Shaye came back to town, she joined his company and he tried to hook up with her again. I got the sense she didn't put him off completely, didn't want to alienate the guy who fixes her computer, but she really wasn't interested in dating him."

"So, how does Grant fit into the picture now?"

"A co-worker hinted he was infatuated with Shaye, and his screensaver is a younger picture of her. He didn't try to hide it. I didn't ask him how he got it, but maybe I need to have another conversation with him?"

"Bottom line, Kathy, do you see him as a suspect?"

She took a sip of coffee, dabbed at her mouth with the blue clothe napkin. Half the egg white omelet lay untouched on her plate, all the toast and mushrooms were gone.

"There is more to this. Grant Ashbury studied the history of the Middle Ages in university, he was into Dungeons & Dragons, the Knights Templar, all that stuff. He's quite proud of it, says a lot of modern science fiction borrows from old traditions and legends and all that." She leaned forward. "He knows a lot about the Stormont dagger." She watched for a reaction.

Brampton was not as impressed as she had hoped. He was mopping up ketchup, grease and egg yolk with a tiny piece of toast. "Did he have *access* to the dagger?"

"Yes! He's seen it several times and knows its full history. I have him on my list of suspects based on the fact he knew both murdered women, but the end of our conversation put him right up there at number one. Listen to this." She fished her iPad out of her bag. "He was fine with me recording the interview, and he seemed to think *this* was a reasonable thing to say."

She hit play at a spot she had queued up. The volume was low, but Brampton felt a chill hearing Ashbury talk about Shaye's noble death and joining women to whom the dagger had brought honour or pain. It was a remarkable thing to say to someone looking into a murder. "Well, that's peculiar," he said drily. "Based on that piece of weirdness, he's definitely a suspect."

"There's more. You know the cold case I'm revisiting, the student who was killed seven years ago, stabbed?"

"I remember you said you were looking into it."

"Dr. Rivers told me the murdered girl, Catrina, worked on a project with a group that included Grant Ashbury."

She leaned forward, elbows on the table, and looked intensely into his eyes. "Catrina handed the project in just before she died," she paused for effect, "or not. Grant had a bit of a rant about her not handing it in on time and how the group lost marks." Brampton's eyebrows rose. "I know, pretty insensitive, but when I talked to Ken, I mean Dr. Rivers, he said she *had* handed it in."

"Ken, eh?" He waggled his eyebrows at her and she blushed. "Interesting. Did you tell Ashbury what he said?"

She slumped back. "No. I wanted to hear how he remembered it, and it's obviously still a touchy subject. He was angry about the unfairness, then realized how that sounded and walked it back. Anyway, it doesn't sound like he had much to do with Catrina, although Rivers suggested he was sweet on her. Grant's a real mix, he got emotional about the lost marks, but he was noncommittal about Catrina. He could be hiding his real memories, or he genuinely had no interest in her, I mean Rivers didn't have any proof, just a feeling."

Brampton considered. "What does your gut say?"

Kathy looked pleased. She believed in her instincts. "The two girls were alike, auburn hair, blue eyes, about the same height, nice figure, well endowed"

Brampton thought back to the latest victim, and to pictures he'd seen of Catrina. Similar body type and coloring, even their hair, long and wavy and worn loose.

"We need to see the old autopsy," said Kathy. "The summary says stabbed once, but they don't say anything about a weapon. Could it have been a dagger? If the cases are linked that way, hell, Grant Ashbury is definitely a prime suspect."

Brampton nodded, dabbed his mouth with his napkin, then clapped his hands together. "Okay, my turn. I'm glad you're sitting down."

20. Brampton's Break-fast Surprise

She was putting her tablet away, sorting out things to leave but she stopped and looked up sharply.

"Why? What's happened?"

"There's a surprising new suspect."

A muscle tightened in her back. "Another suspect? Oh lord. I thought we had two prime suspects in Deborah and Grant, now you say there's a third?"

"A strong one." He was pleased to have her attention so completely. "I wanted to know who paid for Shaye Alderson's funeral. It was pretty basic, medium-priced, but there's no immediate family, and this is a murder investigation, so I called the funeral home. Fred Falcone's place, do you know him?" Kathy shook her head. "I do, and he was happy to fill me in. Hold onto your hat."

Kathy could see he was enjoying himself. She waited patiently for his big reveal.

"Shaye has a half-sister, Madeline Saunders," he said. "A long lost, newly found half-sister."

"Okay," said Kathy slowly. "That's news. Why is she a suspect?"

"They only found out about each other two years ago and met for the first time last year. Madeline Saunders is in rough financial shape, lots of money worries, so I'm not sure how she paid for the funeral."

"And that makes her a suspect?" Kathy asked.

He nodded. "Seems Shaye changed her will to leave all

her worldly goods to this Madeline, a small investment account, her house and car, about half a million bucks when it's liquidated."

"Wow, even without financial trouble that would be a motivator," said Kathy, adding, "for the wrong person."

She relaxed back into the red leatherette booth and raised three fingers. "So now we've got three deadly sins as possible motives." She tapped her index finger. "Lust! Call it passion, for Grant." She tapped her middle finger. "Envy for Deborah who desperately wanted Shaye's position at work." She tapped her ring finger. "Greed from this new character, Madeline Saunders." She put her elbow on the table, rested her chin on the three fingers. "And any one of them could be our murderer."

Brampton pushed his empty plate aside looking thoughtful. Kathy spoke. "Where does she live, this Madeline? I can go and have a chat with her. What do you think?"

"If you're willing, that would be great. "I'm reluctant to bring in a grieving relative for questioning, not without good cause. I have no idea if she knew about the will, so before I make headlines by dragging in a weeping sister, I'd appreciate you talking to her."

"Give me her address and phone number," said Kathy, waggling the three fingers at Sandy. "I'll call and set up a meeting."

21. Suspect Madeline Saunders

Kathy phoned ahead to set up a meeting. Sometimes showing up unannounced worked well, other times it thrust people into defensive mode. She made it clear she was investigating Shaye's untimely death.

Madeline Saunders had been gruff, belligerent even, on the phone and Kathy was careful not to push. She sympathized with her loss, was apologetic about bothering her, explained her interest in the case, leaving out the fact that she'd actually found the body, and assured the woman she would not stay long. It was a three-hour drive, but Kathy knew it had to be face to face.

As Kathy hung up, she wondered the chilly attitude usually meant the woman had something to hide.

She was happy driving down the highway, pleased to be leaving the city. She took a detour onto a road that ran parallel to the highway so she could go slower and enjoy the view of open fields and crops. There might even be some horses. It was summer, a fine, clear day.

She rolled down the window and enjoyed the breeze in her hair. She thought about Sandy Brampton. He was such a nice person, and she could feel his interest in her. She noticed when he moved toward her, as if he was going to touch her, then stopped himself. Could they take their relationship to the next level, wander off in the direction of romance? Someday she would have to find out.

When she reached Kingston, she maneuvered her way through unfamiliar streets until she found Smith Falls Avenue. She drove almost to the end, slowing down to read the numbers and stopped outside 233, a small, rather shabby brick bungalow.

Outside the car she smoothed her skirt, grabbed her purse and took a moment to slip into her objective interviewer mild neutral posture. Madeline might be watching.

As she neared the door, sure enough she saw a young woman standing a little way back from the open door, behind an old screen door, watching her approach. Pleasant looking, brown hair pulled back in a neat bun, she wore a grey nurse's uniform but her feet were bare. She pushed open the screen door.

"Hello Kathy, I'm Madeline Saunders." Kathy noticed the casual use of her first name and the more formal introduction of herself. "Please come in and have a seat."

The living room was drab but tidy, a loveseat and two armchairs arranged on a peach paisley rug – identical to the one in Shaye Alderson's cottage, minus the bloodstains.

22. Suddenly Sisters

Kathy blinked at the carpet and followed Madeline's nod toward a plump green armchair. Before she could speak, the other woman began.

"I want to apologize for sounding rude on the phone. I'd just walked in the door. I'm a surgical nurse and I'd just finished my shift when an auto accident victim came in." She drew breath. "A young girl. We worked six hours on her, but in the end, we lost her. I was very tired." Her eyes flashed, "Some stupid kid racing his father's car. He had only minor scrapes."

That explained the coldness on the phone, exhaustion that sounded like hostility.

"I completely understand, and I'm sorry if I sounded vague when we spoke, but your sister's death is proving to be a real mystery and I'm absorbed by it."

Madeline's gaze was steady. "It's all very unsettling. Murder is awful, senseless. Why would anyone take a life? I see a lot of death, unnecessary death. It happens." She tipped her head back and studied the ceiling, then patted her knees as she let out a sigh. "Never mind, how can I help."

"Tell me about your relationship with Shaye."

Madeline nodded and sat back, hands folded in her lap. "It's complicated. If you've done your homework you know we only just discovered each other. You see, I was the product of a four-day conference." She paused and made a face. "This is not coming out well, bear with me.

My mom was a single mother and I never knew my dad. She never talked about him, just told me he was dead," she gave a hard little laugh, "and I was expected not to think about it, just get on with life like she did. I grew up here in Kingston, went to University in Toronto, lived and worked there for a while. I got married to a wonderful man and when he got a job in Kingston, I found a position at the hospital here, so we moved back. Then just over two years ago my mom got sick. Cancer," she sighed.

"She was stage four when they diagnosed it. She used to joke she'd worked all her life for it, lung cancer," she tapped her chest. "Mom was a big-time smoker and she went downhill fast. When she learned she had just a few weeks to live she said she had something to tell me."

She stopped again and stared at nothing over Kathy's shoulder. Kathy wondered if she was playing for time. Madeline came back to the present and continued.

"She told me about the time she went away with two friends to a resort in Huntsville. They were nurses, worked long hours and had no money, no boyfriends, so when one of them won a weekend away, they all went and squeezed into one room, probably their idea of luxury. There was a sales conference at the hotel, lots of handsome, smart young men and," she spread her hands and smiled, "she fell for one. I guess they had their stolen moments and I was the result.

"He was married so she must have been pretty dumb, and he wasn't very responsible, but she didn't sound bitter when she told me." She looked squarely at Kathy. "In fact, she sounded happy. Me? I felt pissed off, to be honest. Cheated. I'd never had any dad stories growing up, not even about my supposedly dead dad."

The coldness had crept back. She squared her shoulders and carried on. "Mom never told him about me, and she never saw him again. He had a wife and family, it would cause them pain. She figured we could survive without him and we did.

"But she came clean before she died, told me she wanted me to find him, but," she closed her eyes for a long moment, "she'd left it too late."

Kathy sat back. This woman was being honest. It was a simple story, told with a rawness that touched her heart.

"I tried to find him and discovered he and his wife had been killed in a car accident. It could have stopped there, but then I discovered Shaye. She was 19 when they died. and she was my sister, okay half sister, but my only blood relative. I had nothing to lose by reaching out. She might be interested in talking to me. Maybe she felt alone, too. I didn't stop to think that it might rock her world." She flicked tears away. "We hit it off right away, she was excited to meet, and so was I. After that first time, we really felt like sisters and did stuff together, lunch and shopping." She tapped the rug with her bare foot. "We bought the same rug one day because it was on sale and we thought it would be fun to have the same carpet."

Her cell phone buzzed, startling them both. "Excuse me please, I have to attend to my husband."

23. Out of the Blue Rich

She left the room. Kathy pondered. Did Madeline know what inheritance Shaye had left her? Was that a motive for murder? It seemed unlikely as Madeline seemed genuinely distraught to be deprived of her sister.

Madeline returned and offered tea or coffee, and Kathy chose tea. She heard her moving about the kitchen, running water, arranging crockery, the whistle of a kettle and then she came back with two flora patterned china mugs on a tray along with a teapot wearing a black and pink striped tea cozy. "My mother was a knitter," she explained. "I've got a ton of these if you want to take one home, any color you like." They both laughed.

"I'm sorry about the interruption but my husband needed attending to."

"Is he ill, or injured?" Kathy asked politely.

"Injured," said Madeline. "He's a mess. An accident at work, broke a leg and his pelvis, concussion, even his hearing was affected. He doesn't remember anything about the accident, which is good because there was nobody around and he didn't get help for about an hour." Her eyes flashed and her voice rose. "The company are being complete bastards, claiming he was drunk on the job, they're refusing to pay compensation. We've exhausted our coverage and he needs specialist treatment we can't afford. I'm sorry, that's more information than you asked for, but it's affected our life – a lot."

Kathy immediately thought her husband's predicament could be a strong motive for murder.

She was usually a good reader of people, but she didn't have a good sense of Madeline yet. It was time to test her.

"Did you know Shaye left you her house and some money?"

Madeline didn't seem to understand. Then her eyes widened and she put her mug down heavily, slopping tea on the tray. "What?" she cried, and clasped her hand over her mouth.

...

Madeline sank back into the cushions looking dazed. Tears trickled down her nose. "Jesus, I had no idea. Why hasn't anyone told me? Are you sure?"

Her shock looked real. Kathy would learn later that Madeline had borrowed against her own life insurance to pay for Shaye's funeral

"Have you not heard from Jeb Stone?" said Kathy, reaching out to touch her knee. "His law firm is handling her estate. Surely he called you?"

Madeline's expression changed. "I did receive a couple of messages from a Jeb Stone QC, but I thought that was to do with my husband's company lawsuit."

Kathy leaned forward and dabbed with a paper napkin at the tea spilled on the tray. "Jeb Stone is a junior lawyer with Jackson, Jackson and Kelsey lawyers."

"I've heard of them," Madeline exclaimed. "If I had known I would have call right back. I guess it's my fault."

"It's a really nice house," Kathy said awkwardly.

"I know, I've been there. It's wonderful. I just can't believe she would leave it to me."

Just then, Madeline's phone chimed. Madeline made an

exasperated sound. "It's time to do some things for my husband. It takes about a half an hour and he gets crabby, I don't know if we can carry on."

Was this being a ploy to get rid of her? Surely Madeline was eager to learn more about her inheritance.

"Is it something I can help with, or is there anything I can do out here for you?"

"Thank you, but no," said Madeline firmly. "We do physical exercises, move his arms and legs to keep the circulation going, and he has to do cognitive exercises, too. He doesn't enjoy it. I'm sorry, but it's really important to keep to his schedule. Maybe we can meet again? I can get someone to sit with him and come to see you if you need to ask me more, or we could talk on the phone?" she looked anxiously toward the bedroom.

Kathy felt a pang of sympathy. It sounded like Mr. Saunders was hard work. There was no way she could politely stay longer. She felt this half-sister was genuine, not a murderer, just a woman trying to get by. The inheritance was good news for her, but the loss of her only blood relation, not so much.

"Let's see how things go in the next week," she said. "If you have to come to talk to Jackson, Jackson and Kelsey we could meet up. I'm looking into everything to do with your sister's death," she added. "It was me who found her."

Madeline looked shocked, but they were out of time. An insistent banging was coming from the bedroom. Kathy mentally slapped herself for dropping a bombshell at the last minute.

At the front door Madeline said, "I knew nothing about this inheritance, the whole thing has been such a shock to me. I discovered I had a sister, we were becoming good friends, then somebody killed her," she drew a ragged, breath and another loud thump came from the bedroom. "I must go," she said, turning away. "Steve's a good man. He didn't deserve this." She turned back. "Shaye was a lovely person; she didn't deserve what happened to her." She turned and walked quickly away.

Kathy stood alone on the porch. She walked to her car, climbed in and drove away, replaying their conversation in her head. Madeline had problems and the inheritance would go a long way toward solving some of them. She was angry with her husband's company, angry that she'd been denied a father, angry to lose her sister to an act of violence. Christ, she was angry to have lost a young girl in the operating room. But Madeline was a nurse, she saved lives. Would she deliberately take one to help her husband?

Kathy felt the beginnings of a headache, but she turned on the radio anyway, tuned into a classical station and settled in for the long drive home.

24. Another Suspect And
A Great Breakfast

For once, Kathy was early for their meeting at Rosy's. The sun was low in the sky, the air fresh and the streets quiet when she pulled into the lot. When she got home from Madeline's house she had found a message from Sandy inviting her to breakfast. She was eager to share what she had learned.

Brampton walked in wearing a white shirt, blue blazer and tan slacks. Seated at their regular table, Kathy checked him out as he approached. She smiled encouragingly as he got closer. Her mind drifted to thoughts of the toned body beneath his clothes and the musky scent of his cologne rather than the reasons for their meeting. It was a pleasant diversion, but she snapped out of it as he slid into his seat. She drummed her fingers on the table to show she was ready for business, but couldn't resist taking a deep breath to feel that musky cologne.

"Good morning, Sandy, how are you?"

"Just wonderful this fine morning, and how are you?" He was thinking she looked even better in the clear morning light and risked putting his hand close to hers. He tapped his own little bump-diddy-bump on the table between them.

She colored slightly. "I'm good, I'm great. Thanks for asking."

Lucy approached and, seeing them focused on each

other, took their orders quickly and left.

Brampton shook out his blue gingham cloth napkin, one of the reasons he frequented Rosy's. He hated those stiff paper napkins that slide off your lap. He got straight to the point. "How did it go with Madeline? Did you learn anything that might be helpful?"

"It was interesting," said Kathy. "She told me how a couple of years ago when her mother was dying, she learned about her biological father. She went looking for him but he was dead, which must have been awfully disappointing." Brampton nodded and made a *can you imagine* face. "Then she found out she had a half-sister. Shaye, which must have been pretty exciting." He thought about making another face, but decided to just nod.

"Did you get the feeling Shaye and her were friends, were they close? What do you think their relationship was?"

Kathy pondered. "She was kind of guarded about everything. Claims they were becoming good friends, best friends, but there was an edge to it. I'm not sure what I was expecting from her, but of course she was going to be broken up. If I learned about my long lost dad, then found he was dead, then found I had a sister, then she gets killed. I don't mean to judge, but Madeline felt a little off to me."

"Did she seem defensive or angry?"

Kathy took a mental step back and thought. "Not exactly. Just guarded. She shed some tears, but that could have been fake." She threw up her hands. "Oh, now I sound cynical." She chewed on her thumbnail and looked up from under her lashes. "I stick with my impression she had her guard up, and she kept it up for most of the meeting."

"Did she know about the inheritance?"

"No," said Kathy firmly. "She claims she knew nothing about it and I believe her. It was one of the few moments she seemed genuinely surprised."

"Surprised that you knew about it, or surprised that she was getting a windfall?"

"Surprised that she was getting an inheritance. She was really taken aback. Sat back in the chair, started to cry, it was like she really let go for a minute and it looked genuine to me. Think about it, she found people, lost them, her husband's all messed up and now she's coming into money." She shook her head slowly.

"Okay," he said briskly. "What about her circumstances, would the money really be a motive?"

Kathy nodded and told him about the accident, the fight with the company, how she was working double shifts to make ends meet. "On the drive home, I realized she hadn't asked how much money was involved."

Brampton agreed that was strange. "Going back to her relationship with Shaye, what did she say about that?"

Kathy recounted what she remembered about the shopping trips, the lunches and phone calls. "She admitted she was resentful that Shaye had known their dad, but I believe she was just glad to have *some* family, and she was sure Shaye was happy to have found her."

"Right," he banged the table making the salt and pepper jump. Kathy jumped, too. "What about your gut? Is she a suspect? Could she be a murderer?"

Kathy laughed. "If I could tell that kind of thing I'd be hiring myself out to your department for big bucks, not meeting you for free at 7:30 in the morning." He laughed and Lucy, cleaning a table beside them, stole a glance and wished she could figure out just what was going on between them.

Kathy held her hands up and said, "Really, I do not know. She might be a good actor. My instinct is she's hiding something. Until I find out what that is, I can't know if she's telling the whole truth about their friendship. For all we know she wanted Shaye dead and the tears are fake – or remorse."

25. Black Pepper and Yogurt

Breakfast arrived. Sandy picked up the black pepper and shook it onto his omelet and hash browns. Through a mouthful of her egg white omelet Kathy asked, "How do you know it needs pepper before you taste it?"

He gave the pepper another deliberate shake before answering. "In all the years I've eaten here I find the omelet bland, it's salty but not as spicy as I like. A touch of pepper jazzes it up." He gave two more defiant shakes and hoped he wouldn't regret it.

"I've got some other news. I have a friend at the hospital where Madeline works and I asked her to get me Madeline's fingerprints."

Kathy looked surprised. "Can you do that? Don't you need a warrant or something?"

He raised a forkful of egg to his mouth, peered at the layer of black pepper, shrugged and popped it in. It was perfect. He blotted his lips with the linen napkin and said reasonably, "If she was a suspect and I was thinking of charging her then, yes, I'd get a warrant. For now I just wanted to identify any of her prints at the scene."

Brampton did things by the book. He was ethical and methodical. Of the two of them, she was the wild card who bent the rules. If he had obtained Madeline's fingerprints, off the record, and was telling her about it, there must be something worth telling.

"Go on then, what's the news?"

"I knew the hospital would have her fingerprints on

file, they keep drugs in a secure area that requires a hand scan to unlock it. As a surgical nurse, she'd have access to the drugs, and we haven't ruled out drugs being part of Shaye's death. We compared her prints to all the prints we got at Shaye's house." Kathy was about to tell him that Madeline had freely admitted visiting the house, but he swept on. "Are you ready for this? Her prints are on the dagger."

Kathy's hand went limp, she'd been holding a spoon heaped with yogurt which splatted onto the tabletop. She reflexively pushed it away from the edge to stop it dripping onto her lap, then used her napkin to clean her hand. "Geeze," she groaned. "That *is* news." She hadn't thought to ask Madeline about the dagger. Why would she?

Brampton watched her clean-up efforts. She looked flustered, but he knew she was thinking hard. He could almost hear the wheels turning.

He blew out a breath. "We've got to get her in for questioning, but maybe you can talk to her again informally?"

Kathy nodded. "I'll talk to her some more. She's got a lot of stress, dealing with some hard stuff. If she's innocent, I don't want to add to her pain, but we got on okay, she seemed agreeable to another conversation. She's not a flight risk, because she can't leave her husband. Let me try."

She thought again of the coldness in Madeline's voice on the phone, then the helpless tears. Was it truly stress, or was she being scammed?

26. Stab Wounds On The Screen

"Off to the dead house, man?" Detective Corey Brown deliberately bumped Brampton as the passed in the hall. He threw two playful punches and got a swat round the head in return.

"You like that lady doc, eh? How can she be so hot in that cold, cold place?" Brampton ignored him, grabbed his iPod and strode out for a meeting with coroner, Linda MacDugon. If Corey Brown was smarter, he'd know the only hot lady in Brampton's thoughts was Kathy Chatsworth. Nevertheless, alone in the elevator, he smoothed his jacket and tidied his hair. The tinted mirrors were flattering. He grinned at Brown's playful goading.

He'd asked MacDugon for more information on the cold case murder of Catrina Somers, pushing past her objections to persuade her to take another look at the seven-year-old report and any evidence in storage.

As he entered the cool examining room, he was grateful to see they were alone. No patients on the gleaming steel tables. Despite ten years dealing with dead bodies, Brampton could never see them as empty vessels. It wasn't a religious thing, probably more to do with watching horror movies as a kid, but even when a corpse had no face to speak of, he was painfully aware it had once been a person. He never volunteered to attend autopsies unless it was critical to a case.

MacDugon was sitting with her eyes closed, buds in her ears and boots on her desk. She looked up as he entered and said caustically, "Revisiting a seven-year-old cold case, this is one of Kathy's wild ideas?"

Straight to the point, he thought. *No hello, how you doing, get right into it and let me know exactly how you feel about it.* "And hello, good morning to you, Linda," he said pleasantly and wheeled a chair up to the desk. He took his time pulling out a notebook and pen, patting his pockets until he found the iPhone. "Yes, it was Kathy's idea, but you know some of her ideas actually turn out to be right."

The coroner laughed and raised her hands in a *you-win* gesture. "She's right just often enough to make me agree to check out her hunches, but don't tell her that. Sometimes her crazy ideas get results, but she's a little intense for me, in fact I think she's a whack job. But when she wanders off into the wild blue yonder she occasionally comes back with something that helps us close a case."

He fought the urge to leap to Kathy's defense. He didn't want MacDugon speculating about their relationship. He gave a noncommittal grunt. At least she agreed they might not be wasting her time.

"Let's go then. Have you had a chance to look at the material, did you find files or data that will help?"

She beckoned for him to wheel his chair round to her side of the desk so he could see her 30-inch screen.

"I have some great new software called Body Scan 500 we can use to scan photographs and then analyze information around stab wounds and bullet holes. It's pretty exciting."

Brampton didn't think he'd enjoy close-ups of bullet holes and stab wounds, but then he wasn't a coroner.

"If we're looking for a connection between the two murders it will let us closely compare the autopsy photographs. This thing is smarter than the naked eye," she grinned. "Even mine."

***

She slid a photograph of Shaye's stab wound on to the scanner plate. The machine hummed and in seconds the image appeared on the large computer screen. She typed in commands and lines of data unrolled on the screen indicating the size of the wound, location on the body, probable entry direction and a number of other elements.

She repeated the process with a photograph of Catrina. The scanner hummed, the picture appeared and Brampton frowned at the sight of slashed flesh.

"Now it's time to have some fun," MacDugon said and cracked her knuckles. "The software can do amazing things. I'll ask it to compare the two stab wounds and let's see what we come up with."

The photos slid smoothly into position side by side, and information balloons began to pop up around them as the body sector technology did its work.

She let out a whistle. "Score one for Kathy, it's interesting."

Brampton was looking at the data and seeing similarities, but he waited for her to explain before he jumped to conclusions.

"The puncture wounds are in almost the identical place on their chests and almost the exact same width. The analysis of the incision shows a high probability the same blade created both wounds. We know the Stormont dagger was used to kill Shaye," she was speaking very seriously now. "It looks like it could have been the murder weapon seven years ago."

27. MacDugon Is Impressed

Brampton took a breath. Kathy had been right. Once again he thought what an interesting person she was, and how glad he was to know her. And once again his thoughts drifted to asking her out, he wondered how she felt about their friendship – then the pictures of cruel stab wounds came back into focus and he shuddered.

"You okay Sandy? You look a little strange." He snapped back and felt MacDugon's hand on his arm. She was peering at him, and he gave his head a shake. "Yes, sorry, just thinking."

She continued. "They're almost ritual, the cuts. First, they're in the same place on the chest, right into the center of the heart. They're both horizontal, east to west rather than north to south. That's unusual. We know the dagger has a bunch of rituals in its history, some crazy-ass ceremony when a rich guy asks a girl to marry them." Brampton couldn't help laughing, but she was not amused. "Do we know if the ritual includes a particular way he's supposed to use it? Is there like a special way to wield the knife?" She shook her head in disgust.

Brampton sat quietly, watching her think.

"Okay," she slapped her knees and stood up. "Kathy needs to look into the ceremony stuff. See if there's anything in the history about how you're supposed to hold the knife, how to strike. Normally if you stab someone in the heat of passion," she snorted, "not that *normally* is the right word, but let's say usually if you plunge a knife into somebody's heart, the cut is north-south which slows it down because it will likely hit the rib cage. The way these wounds went, the blade slid between the second and third ribs and stabbed quick and deep into the heart. That motion would drive straight to the heart and cause it to rupture. Death would come in seconds. Pain would be minimal."

Kathy, the nosey journalist, was the perfect person to ask questions about the history of the dagger without tipping anyone's hand there was evidence linking two murders.

Gordon Stormont had touched on details of the bizarre ceremony, but Brampton was not a history buff. He'd listened in a half-hearted way, thinking more about the present than the past. It was Kathy who obsessed on the bits and pieces of a story and picked up on obscure information with her 'wild blue yonder' thinking.

MacDugon was talking again. "One of the weird things about Catrina's murder is why the killer put her on the bed, covered her with a duvet. At first we figured it was done to shift the time of the murder. A duvet would have kept the body warmer making it more difficult to pinpoint time of death. Now I wonder if it could be part of this fucking ceremony." The coroner was blunt and could be rude but she rarely swore. "Calling it a ceremony is just nonsense, but if there *are* instructions on how to kill a woman who rejects your proposal we need to know what they are. If the dagger's history was in play for these murders, we need to find out more."

She stood and held out her hand to him, making it clear his time was up.

In the car, he scribbled notes and mused on how Dr. MacDugon was now fully engaged in the investigation.

She was no longer skeptical about Kathy's ideas. He'd seen her mild irritation at having to revisit an old case turn into real anger on behalf of the murdered women. Maybe she *did* feel the humanity of the dead but was just good at hiding it.

28. Dagger and Other Rituals

Kathy picked up on the first ring. "Hi Sandy, how are you today?"

He resisted the urge to dive right in and replied with exaggerated civility, "I'm doing just fine Kathy, and how are you?" *Talk about rituals*, he thought.

"Just peachy, thanks for asking," she said with a fake Southern accent. That was the politeness game out of the way. "Did you dig into that cold case?"

"Yep," he said. "Score one for you and your instincts. Linda has new computer modeling or recognition or whatever they call it that compares wounds and she's 99% sure the dagger that killed Shaye was used on Catrina Somers. "

Kathy let out the breath she'd been holding. "Wow. That's great news. Oh dam, I don't mean that, it's awful that someone slaughtered two women and they're still out there. We've got to stop it happening again!"

Brampton agreed. "We might think the whole dagger history thing is nonsense, but it's clearly part of what's happening here. I need your help finding out more about this so-called ceremony. Are there other bloodletting rituals, why is the dagger so important, are there rituals around how it's used?"

Kathy frowned. "You mean physically how it's used? I don't understand."

Brampton slowed it down. "Okay, let's think about this. By definition a ritual has procedures, the order in which you do things, what you use, what you say, there's rules for everything from satanic rituals to the bloody boy scouts. Linda established the knife cuts were horizontal, she said east to west and in almost the exact same place, between the second and third ribs. Coincidence? Unlikely."

Kathy felt a tremor of excitement. "I can find out! I'll start with Rivers, he loves any excuse to talk about this stuff. I can ask Grant and Deborah, too, they're both obsessed with the dagger's history, I wonder how much they know about the less savory aspects of it? Oh, sorry, was this something you wanted to do?"

He chuckled. "God no, I was hoping you'd volunteer. Those people already know you're interested in the history of the thing, hopefully it won't ring any alarm bells if you go back with more questions." He grinned, thinking of Linda's description of Kathy as a whack job. She wasn't the only one in this case. "We'll keep it quiet that we've linked the two cases, don't want to alert the murderer."

Kathy considered what her approach should be. Everyone knew the dagger was the murder weapon in the death of Shaye. It was not unreasonable to ask more questions, and they were all proud to show off what they knew about the thing.   *And Grant Ashbury knew both women, too,* she thought with a shudder.

"Give me a couple of days, I'll figure out a way to talk to Rivers and Grant again. I should go back to Gordon Stormont, too, but he's out of the country for a couple of weeks and I don't want to wait that long to get started."

Brampton agreed but cautioned her, "Go careful, Kathy. Remember they were young attractive women and somebody stabbed them. It's starting to look like some sort of ceremonial revenge, but we don't know that. You're a young, attractive woman." He paused and swallowed hard. "I don't want you to risk being corpse number three."

Kathy smiled at her end of the call. "Got it. I'll be super careful, and thanks for your concern." *Young and attractive*, she thought with a flush of pleasure. "I won't mention the cold case, just ask about the dagger's history and the ceremony. It's horrible but fascinating, all those men following a crazy blood-letting ritual, even the ones who thought it was hogwash, and as for the ones who actually killed a woman they supposedly loved." She threw caution to the wind. "I guess I'm lucky nobody loves me."

Brampton held the phone away from his ear and stared at it. He grinned but didn't take the bait. "Just be careful. Keep me posted, I've got your back."

She wasn't sorry she'd said it. She had heard his hesitation. "I know Sandy. I know. I'll stay in touch. Have a lovely day with no more murder and mayhem in it."

29. Back To Professor Rivers

Kathy was still practicing once a week with Deborah at the fight club, and they occasionally went for coffee after the session – it would be a perfect time to ask more about the strange rituals around the dagger. Deb was a little eccentric, but she enjoyed her company and fervently hoped her new friend was *not* involved in the murders. She was sure Grant would be glad to talk more about the dagger, but before Grant she wanted to go back to Dr. Rivers, to Ken, she reminded herself and grinned. She thought about Brampton's admiration for Linda Mac-Dugon's computer skills, and grinned some more. *She* didn't need any fancy software to do her work, just good old-fashioned research and people skills.

By mid-morning she had set up a call with Rivers for 3:30 that day. She rang at 3:28 and he answered promptly. "Kathy, how nice to hear from you again. What can I do for you?"

"Nice to hear your voice, too," she said sweetly and imagined him preening. "I have some more questions about the history of the Stormont dagger, I know it's short notice but do you have time for a chat now?"

His enthusiasm was obvious. "Not a problem. It's a real pleasure to talk about history, any history, to someone who is genuinely interested. In fact, it's what we old professors dream about."

She rolled her eyes, but kept the smile in her voice. "Oh

yes, I'm fascinated by this macabre tradition. I want to know more about how the ceremony unfolds. Is there a set procedure, a ritual to follow? Does one do things in a certain order? Just what goes on in the whole process?"

For the next hour, Ken walked Kathy through the whole ceremony, the physical preparations, the most propitious environment, variations and rules, all the details. The ceremony was based on disciplines from hundreds of years ago, when the world was very different. No doubt it had been tweaked over the centuries, but the old ways were the foundation of the rituals, and certain things had to be done *just so*.

Kathy's head was spinning with colourful stories, meandering detours and unrelated anecdotes when Ken grew silent. "Of course, we have *not* talked about what happens if the lady rejects the man. Did you know he has the option of killing her?" He listened for her reaction, but all he heard was a soft, "Oh!"

"I have to go to a class now," he said. "But if you call me Friday, I'll tell you all about it. I hadn't meant to talk for so long, but I was enjoying myself. Sorry, but I really must go."

Kathy curled her hands into fists and pounded her knees in silent frustration. "No worries," she said brightly. "I'll get back to you Friday or beginning of next week." She was careful not to let him sense how desperate she was to hear about that killing option.

30. Deb Gets Serious

Sweat was running down her face, it was the hardest workout yet and she was in a certain amount of pain, but as she rose gingerly from the mat, she told herself it was worth it. Since joining the club she'd lost five pounds and certainly had more energy.

She and Deb had sparred last, they bowed to each other at the end then Deb broke the formality by trilling in a fake, posh accent, "Shall we have a nice cup of tea, darling?"

Kathy laughed. "Oh let's! And I wouldn't mind talking to you about those crazy ceremonies around the Stormont dagger. Do you mind?"

"Hell, no." Deborah was back to her own voice. "I'm flattered you would ask, but can't Gordon Stormont can tell you that stuff?"

Kathy explained he was away and she was eager to finish the draft of her article on the death of Shaye.

After Deb's shower and her usual shouted conversation from behind the curtain, they made their way to their regular Tim Horton's coffee shop. It was Kathy's turn to buy the teas, while Deb grabbed a bench by the window.

"Ah thanks, Kath, it's good tea, but I kind of wish we were drinking wine." They both liked a glass of wine now and then, but after such a punishing workout, hot tea was the wiser choice. "So, you want to know about the ceremony. The whole story? It's long and weird, or is there a particular part you're curious about?"

Kathy pretended to think. "Gordon told me about the basic ceremony, how a gentleman presents the dagger, the lucky lady accepts it and holds it a certain way and then they're officially betrothed. I heard that if she doesn't want to marry him, she refuses to take the dagger, and that means she's rejecting him. But then I heard another part that he has the right to attack her if she rejects him?" She feigned confusion. "What's *that* about?"

"It's interesting," said Deborah mildly. "Part of it is oral history, passed down in the family, but some of it is actually written down. I've heard there's a really old document somewhere, one of those illuminated things that monks did, with hand painted pictures and gold leaf and everything. I've never seen it, I've only seen the boring modern typed-up version, but, yes, I can tell you the written down rules."

Deborah took a sip of tea and gathered her thoughts. Kathy was watching for signs of discomfort, something that would lead to suspicion, but she had to admit she couldn't really read Deborah.

It seemed as if Deb was reading her thoughts, though. "Sorry, I'm just thinking and trying to remember. It's been a while since I even thought about the story." Kathy doubted that. "Actually, the Stormont dagger is one of the reasons I got involved with the club and learning combat knife skills."

She took another sip of tea, sat back and spread her arms along the top of the booth looking straight at Kathy. *She's deciding how to say something,* Kathy thought.

When she spoke, there was an almost pleading note in her voice, as if she knew what she was saying was not quite right. "Remember these rituals were set up hundreds of years ago, when men totally dominated their women. Women were like chattels. They rarely owned anything, unless they were very smart or had influence

with a powerful man. Their wealth went to their hus-
bands, and they had very little say what they did with it."

She paused, then went on in a rush, "Okay, I'm just
going to jump right in. If a woman rejected a Stormont
man, he could choose to release her or take her life." She
paused again and Kathy made a strangled little noise. "I
know, it's brutal, eh? But back then they seemed to think
it was romantic, even noble, like if they couldn't have
the woman, they thought was their one true love, they
wouldn't let anyone else have her. There's a clue right
there, they wanted to possess her, so they'd rather kill
her."

Deborah stopped to judge the effect on Kathy, who
widened her eyes and murmured "Jesus Christ. Go on."

"This next part sounds awful, but there are still a lot of
crazy religious rituals done around the world today, most
of them against women of course," Deb said through
clenched teeth. "You can just about understand a crime
of passion, but if a Stormont guy chose to kill a woman
for rejecting him, he was obliged to follow precise guide-
lines, which is even more fucked up. He had to hold her
at the back of her neck and pull the right side of her body
against his so she couldn't raise her arm. Then he stabbed
her between the second and third ribs on the left side to
drive the dagger straight into her heart." She shook her
head sadly.

For someone so enamored of knives and rites and
rituals, Deb seemed genuinely disturbed that there was
a "right" way to stab someone. Or was she reliving the
moment? She put down her tea. "Okay, the next part is
interesting. They're holding her neck, they've driven the
dagger into her heart, then they're supposed to pull the
knife out "full smoothe and quick." That's smooth with

an "e", I remember that's how it was written. They don't say why, that's just what's written down in the book. And then someone later told me that lets the blood escape fast which means she dies faster which, I guess, is a blessing."

Who the hell does Deb know that has tips for how to make someone die faster? Kathy wondered.

"Now here's the kicker," said Deb, on a roll now. "Having killed the woman he supposedly loves and can't bear to live without," she made a gagging noise, "or more honestly killed a woman he can't bear to allow to go on living, he is supposed to lay her down gently and hold her till she dies. The old woman I talked to about this suggested that was to force the man to face what he'd done, that they can't just be pissed off, stab her and run away. They're supposed to understand there is honor involved and the rules, the code, says they're honor-bound to stay and hold her and watch the life seep out of her." She snorted. "Because that will make them think twice before choosing to kill her. Do you think? I don't. Anyway, all the honor crap doesn't help the woman after the fact."

Kathy was taking it all in. She had the odd feeling that this stuff contained a sort of feminine logic. Perhaps somewhere in the dagger's history a woman with a knowledge of anatomy had added a part to the ceremony – a quick death part.

"Then there's the curse," Deb was saying. "If the man stabs in the wrong direction, or doesn't hold her properly as she dies, or if the woman actually escapes – nice to know they took account of that possibility – or if she takes too long to die," she rolled her eyes in disgust, "the man is *cursed*. He is cursed and his family is cursed and all his enterprises will fail forever." She emphasized the last word, then laughed, "to which I say GOOD!"

31. Kathy Maybe Cursed

Kathy thought back to the day she discovered the dagger in the vines. Did the curse explain why it had been thrown away? Shaye had fallen and banged her face on a coffee table, so obviously the killer hadn't held her gently as she died. Kathy had done that. Maybe they panicked and threw away the knife hoping to escape the curse. Brampton said this case was complex – he didn't know the half of it.

Deborah was gathering her things. She took a last sip of tea. "I am fascinated by the Stormont dagger. I've written about it, I've held it, I find it so very interesting but," she shuddered, "I kind of hate it now, too. Gun lovers like to say it's not guns that kill, it's people that kill. I'm not interested in guns but you know I love knives, and I guess you could say the same thing. A weapon isn't evil, it's the person that wields it." She hoisted her bag onto her shoulder. "But you have to wonder, can you actually have an evil knife? Can a knife really carry a curse? Brrrr!" She shook herself but was laughing now. "Do we need a Q and A, or did I cover everything?"

"That's more information than I expected, and now there's a *curse* involved? Why on earth would the family keep the damned thing around?"

Deborah sat back down and clutched her hair dramatically. "Wait! *You* held Shaye as she was dying!" she gripped Kathy's arm. "Does that make *you* part of the ceremony? You have to talk to Gordon right away, find out what this means for you. Are you cursed? Does it even *affect* women? They say it affects the whole family." She had started out joking but now looked genuinely concerned. "Seriously, this is worrying. Talk to Gordon."

Kathy sat very still. She hadn't thought about her involvement. She had been a good Samaritan, she'd tried to help the poor girl and she was helping to find her killer, but was she now mixed up in a messed up, ancient ceremony and a curse?

She didn't believe in curses. But then she'd never been threatened by one before. She suddenly *really* wanted that glass of wine. She wanted to know which side of the curse she was on. She was a good woman. She'd held a dying woman and would have saved her if she could. Surely the stupid Stormont rules didn't include cursing Kathy Chatsworth!

Deborah was watching her. "Hey, lighten up. We'll talk about something else. I didn't mean to freak you out."

Kathy managed a smile. "It's freaky but intriguing. I'm not really worried, but I will definitely talk to Gordon. Go on then, pick a subject. Let's talk about baseball. The Blue Jays," she made a face. "We live in hope, eh?"

For the next half hour, they talked about sports, work and the Blue Jays' dismal performance, but Kathy's mind was churning. Deborah had been very forthcoming. She sure knew a lot about the ceremony, and about Shaye's death, too. How did she know Kathy had held Shaye? Was that in the newspaper?

Her mind rolled over the information, halting at key points then racing on. Deb was still a suspect, but how did another woman fit into the legend? Deb hadn't asked Shaye to marry her. Or had she? She let out a sigh, which stopped Deborah mid-flow as she was sharing ingredients for meatloaf. She gently rubbed Kathy's arm. "Hey, come on. Don't dwell on it."

Kathy sighed again. The legend was getting to her. She'd only held the dagger for a moment but she thought about it constantly. The knife couldn't be the *cause* of any murders. It was shrouded in mystery and history, but it was still just a weapon, cold and inert. The killer was a human being, with possibly no connection to the legend at all. She couldn't wait to get home to that glass of wine.

32. How To Stab Correctly

Two days later she had recovered her good spirits. Long, busy days at work had driven thoughts of Shaye, Catrina and the dagger from her mind.

As she drove to her meeting with Grant Ashbury, she relished the warm day and wondered if this was the day she would catch a killer.

He had welcomed her call, said he was looking forward to sharing what he knew about the rituals.

To prepare for the meeting she had explored his online presence and found his Pinterest account had a section devoted to the beach at Channel Lane Point. That startled her, until she remembered it was a popular beach destination as well as a murder scene.

Ashbury had hundreds of photographs of people on the beach, the delicate part was most of them were young women lying in the sand or walking the beach in their bikinis. Many were close ups.

His other boards had fewer photos and included landscapes, sunsets, still lifes and medieval weapons, including ten pictures of daggers. Five of them were of the Stormont dagger.

Her friend Susan was on the reception desk.

"You again!" Susan said teasingly. "How *are* you?"

"Another day in paradise," Kathy said with a laugh.

"Mr. Ashbury left a message for you," Susan flipped the pages of her memo pad.

Kathy filled in the register and posed for the ID badge

camera. The machine spit out a visitor's badge with the usual awful picture of a startled criminal with no eyebrows. She clipped it to her blouse pocket.

"Mr. Ashbury will meet you in the cafeteria. I sent him a text when I saw you arrive, so he'll be there waiting."

The company cared about its employees and the cafeteria was one of their perks. Floor to ceiling windows flooded it with natural light, special coating kept out UV rays and heat but let in spectacular views of manicured lawns and the forest beyond.

Grant greeted her and looked like he was coming in for a hug, but she stuck out her hand and shook his firmly. He took it well, but placed his hand on her waist to lead her to a table.

:Sorry to trouble you but I really am interested in the dagger ceremony," Kathy said.

"I'm looking forward to this," he said. "It's always interesting to talk about the dagger, so this is no trouble at all. We'll go to the corporate lounge which should be empty at this time of day."

"Corporate lounge?" she said, "that sounds special."

He chuckled. "It was designed for the execs, but now it's open for any employees to retreat to if they need to work on ideas during lunch. From the cafeteria they can come in here, maybe call others in without losing momentum by having to return to an office."

"Smart use of the space," Kathy nodded approvingly.

"Exclusivity out, inclusivity in," he said. "It benefits the company more this way than having senior staff linger over lunch. It gets used for ad hoc meetings or serious thinking that needs quiet or privacy, and it's got a whiteboard so you don't have to scribble ideas on a paper napkin."

Kathy smiled at his enthusiasm and had to agree it was a good place to hang out. They settled into soft leather loveseats facing each other across a low table that held snacks in a big shallow bowl.

"Grant, I'm here because you know so much about the dagger and its rituals," she began. He saluted her with a pretzel. "I want my story to be accurate. I would ask Gordon Stormont for more details, but he's away, so I hope you don't mind indulging me?" She smiled prettily.

"Not at all, and I don't mind being second choice," he joked as he woke his iPad and scrolled.

"I've got original notes from when I first studied the dagger," he was peering at the screen. "The proposal ceremony is quite elaborate, do you want to go through the whole thing?" he glanced up questioningly.

She leaned forward trying to see his screen and he instinctively drew back then looked embarrassed.

"Right now I'm interested in what happened if a woman rejected a Stormont man's proposal."

He narrowed his eyes and studied her for a moment, cleared his throat and began. "The legend is very old, probably adapted from a tale brought back from the Holy Lands along with the gemstone. Someone wrote down the details of the ceremony a couple of hundred years ago, but before that it had been passed down orally. No doubt there were changes to the rituals, and as times changed I'm sure the family saw fit to adapt, but here is what I know.

"Having offered the knife to his intended, the man steps close and takes the knife back with his right hand. He holds the blade down beside his right leg. He places his left hand on her shoulder and again formally asks for her hand in marriage. If she refuses and he accepts her answer he will hold the knife briefly to his own breast, bow low, and take his leave." He watched her closely as he continued.

"If he does not accept her refusal, he has the option to take her life." He paused and waited for her reaction.

Kathy gasped, then swallowed hard. "Go on."

"If he chooses that option, he is to swiftly raise the dagger and stab her between the second and third ribs on her left side, driving the dagger into her heart."

Kathy flinched, and Grant looked gratified which irritated her, but she said in a small voice, "Oh dear, this is fascinating."

Ashbury glanced at his iPad as if to check the next step. "He uses his left arm to hold the girl and lay her on the ground. Something to do with chivalry I believe, cradle her respectfully as she dies, don't just make a quick exit left." His flippancy was inappropriate, considering the recent murder, but Kathy let it pass.

"The legend is quite specific, if he *doesn't* show the proper respect and hold the woman and all that, he will be cursed. I'm afraid I don't know what the curse entails, but it's generally unwise to ignore them," he said seriously and then, unexpectedly, he laughed.

33. Grant's Photographs

In the silence that followed, Kathy thought, *Catrina Somers was placed in bed and covered up lovingly. Respect.* But if Shaye's murder was part of the twisted ritual, the killer had bungled it badly. She fell and struck her face on a coffee table and was left to die alone. If the killer believed the legend, they would know they were cursed.

Kathy ran through the suspects. Deborah, who despised Shaye, would not be inclined to stay and hold her. Madeline, the long lost sister, was unaware of the bizarre history, or was she? Ashbury knew what spoiling the ritual could mean to a believer, but he might still have panicked, forgotten about the honor part and fled. He didn't strike Kathy as a brave man.

As she ran through scenarios in her head, Ashbury went on talking about the ceremony. When she regained her focus, he was insisting that contemporary Stormonts concentrated on the more romantic aspects and certainly didn't inflict *all* the gory details on their fiancés.

"Well that is enthralling," she said, hoping he wouldn't hear her revulsion. "Thank you for sharing it with me." She tapped notes into her laptop and closed the lid, then fanned herself with a hand. "Phew! Enough of that for now."

Shifting gears, she asked about his photography. "I noticed you have several boards on Pinterest about photography. Is that a hobby?"

"Oh, I got into that in high school. It seemed like a good

way to meet girls," he said jauntily, but his cheeks colored.

"I was a bit of a poser, wearing cameras around my neck, but I was genuinely interested and quite good at it. At university the girls were more adventurous and I did some nude photography. After the novelty wore off I could see I wasn't getting anything special, but I *was* fascinated by the human body. I studied classical drawings and sculptures and took a class on anatomy in school."

Kathy filed that away. He would know exactly where to stab a girl to go straight to the heart.

"I like the human form, and you'll see from my beach shots I like to capture casual stuff, people being comfortable in a natural environment. I love the way sunlight hits the body and highlights flesh and bone."

Had Shaye been one of the adventurous girls? Kathy decided to press her luck. "Did the girls at university know you were keeping pictures of them?" she asked nonchalantly.

Ashbury was taken aback. "Absolutely! I was in my romantic phase, or so I thought. I wasn't very good, but I *was* sincere. There was no social media then, so I wasn't posting them anywhere. I kept them for my private collection, but I always gave them copies if they asked."

Kathy nodded amiably. "Do you still have the pictures?"

"They're in an album somewhere," he said vaguely. "I've thought about scanning them, but they're from a time when I was a different person. I wanted to be an artist, but I'm destined to be a tech nerd." He'd regained his humor. "Those pictures are relics of the past," he said dismissively and reached for a pretzel.

It was time to ask about Catrina. "Were the girls all good friends? I don't think I'd have been so brave when I was at university," she said. "Although it would be nice to have a picture to show my kids I was once young and fit." They both laughed.

"I knew most of them from class," he agreed, "Or my study groups, or friends of friends. That's how I shot Catrina." Kathy jumped at the word, then felt foolish.

"She first came along with another girl and then decided to have her own session."

"Are we talking about the same Catrina? The one in your study group and the one who . . .," Kathy hesitated, and he finished for her.

"Died? Yes," he said. "That was so sad. I didn't know her well, but I liked her. Actually, I took pictures of her out at the Channel Lane Point cottage she was renting. I'd forgotten all about that. It was probably about a week before she died."

Kathy sat up straighter. "Wow," it came out involuntarily. *Steady Kathy.* "I, um, I saw you had some pictures of a little cottage. *Don't sound too interested.* "It's a pretty place, eh?"

He was unconcerned. "Let me see. The first pictures I took of Catrina were on the beach and she made a good model, but something went wrong in the developing. The pictures were awful, blurred and blotchy. She suggested we reshoot indoors, and that cottage had beautiful light. *She* actually suggested doing some nudes," his head was down. "She wasn't comfortable outdoors, but she was interested in trying it inside. So having to do a reshoot was not such a bad thing." He seemed unconcerned that he was speaking so lightly of a girl who was murdered about a week later.

34. Kathy Keeps Her Focus

Kathy kept her expression neutral. He'd 'forgotten' that he'd had an intimate photo session with Catrina days before she died. Her jaw tensed, the pretzel she was holding snapped, but Ashbury didn't notice.

Kathy brushed crumbs from her lap. "Did you ever see anybody else at the cottage with Catrina?" It was an awkward moment, the question sounded like an interrogation and he turned back sharply. She mentally kicked herself, but tipped her head and smiled innocently.

"I don't remember," he said stiffly. "Maybe. She had a few suitors, but nobody springs to mind."

Kathy nodded and reached for her bag, then sat back as if she'd just had a thought. "I'd like to look at your pictures some time, if you're open to that. Did you know I'm a judge for amateur photo contests the magazine runs at the high schools? The kids like seeing older film-based stuff, and you could be an inspiration to them."

He studied her for a moment. "Might be interesting. I could let you see some. I don't have them with me of course so we'll have to have another date. I really wouldn't want to bring them into work, could I could bring them to your office?"

"Good idea. Our conference room has good light and is closed off from the main office. We'll be private there, no one can see in." He looked happy with that.

"Does next week work for you? I can get some sorted out by then."

His bland good humour had returned and Kathy was relieved. She had probed a little, he hadn't shut down. He was willing to show and tell her more.

"Absolutely! Let me know when you can make it, I'll provide coffee and doughnuts." She asked one more question. "Did you take any recent photographs of Shaye?"

His mouth tightened and she was reminded of that corporate mask, but then he smiled, "Sadly I didn't. The last ones I took of her were on the beach some time ago. I never got around to asking her approval to post them, so you won't have seen them online. They're not nudes," he added hastily. "Just Shaye at the beach, in a bikini."

Kathy filed this away. From what she'd seen, he often used a long lens, so his subjects wouldn't necessarily be aware they were being photographed.

Two women had entered the room and were perched on nearby chairs, waiting for the comfy couches to be free. As he stood up, Ashbury gestured grandly to the vacant couches. His hand was again on Kathy's waist as they headed for the door, and she resisted the urge to pull away.

...

Standing beside her car in the sunshine, she frowned. Grant Ashbury was pleasant enough, but something about him gave her the creeps. She'd go over it all on the drive home.   She turned the key in the ignition, flipped open her glove compartment and pawed through the contents looking for snacks. She was disappointed when all she found was a bag of stale airline pretzels.

35. Beating The Curse

After her discussion with Deb Citlali, when they had both been spooked by the curse, Kathy emailed Gordon Stormont. She didn't believe in curses, she told him. She didn't believe in ghosts, either, but had always felt it prudent not to tempt fate by boasting about it.

She recalled the night she spent in an allegedly haunted house with a cub reporter. The teenager had started the night making wisecracks, he'd shouted taunts and challenged the spirits to show themselves, but he'd ended the night shivering in Kathy's arms, feeling icy blasts, hearing whispers and crying with fear. She had kept her skepticism to herself that night, and ever since.

She didn't believe in curses, but ...

Gordon Stormont had not laughed at her concerns. He assured her he would find the old family book that held details of the rituals and share the information with her.

As she drove away from her meeting with Ashbury, munching on old pretzels, her phone pinged and she pulled over to check the message. Gordon was back and had found the old book. "Come to the house as soon as possible," he wrote. "Want to share what I found."

Her stomach lurched. Whether because of his urgent tone or the dry salty mass in her mouth she couldn't tell.

...

The butler greeted her at the imposing front door and led her down the hallway. Stormont was sitting in a sunny breakfast room, in front of a very large, very old book propped on a reading stand.

"Kathy, how lovely to see you!" He looked tanned and rested. *How different his business trips must be to mine*, she thought.

"Likewise," she replied. "Sorry to bother you, but I *am* a little worried about what this curse means for me." She gave a little laugh but her eyes were serious.

He gestured to a chair beside him and, when she was seated, leaned forward and carefully turned a page of the book. He wore thin white cotton gloves and held the book steady with one hand as he turned the brittle, parchment page.

"Here we are. The good news is you're on the *upside* of the curse, if there is such a thing. If the man bolts and leaves the woman to die on her own, he is cursed with bad luck for eternity – he and his family and their descendants. I knew that part, but studying the book today I found parts I hadn't read.

A passage had been added at a later date. "It's set apart from the main tract about the curse that befalls the man who dishonors the tradition. It deals with the consequences for everyone concerned if someone *helps* the woman after she is stabbed. The fact that there is this addendum must mean some women were attacked but survived. Of course, these variations would only apply if the ritual is botched or interrupted or otherwise sullied. If it's done correctly and the woman dies, there's no need for them."

Kathy opened her mouth to respond, but thought better of it.

"Ah, here it is, a passage on how the curse manifests itself if another woman holds her as she dies." He pointed to her with a flourish. "That would be *you!*"

He paused. Kathy hoped it was for dramatic effect, and not because something shocking was to follow, but he smiled and resumed.

"The exact words are "she who holds the maid gently as Life leaves her body and her Soul ascends to Heaven will be blessed with goode luck in finding a Goode Man who truly loves her." He traced the words with a gloved finger. "Let me see, blah blah, yes, here it is, "she will have goode fortune and go with grace and her Family, too, shall be blessed for as long as they walk in the paths of Humility and Righteousness."

Kathy noisily let out the breath she had been holding. She repeated the quaint language, particularly the part about "finding a Goode Man." She thought about Sandy Brampton and the way his eyes changed color slightly depending on his mood. She thought about how he occasionally touched her hand, and she thought how nice it would be to have him sitting with her right now. She smiled at Gordon Stormont, and he smiled back.

"Good," she said a little gruffly. "Good stuff. Thank you, Gordon. Thank you so much. I have more questions, but give me a second until I can breathe again!"

"Were you *really* so worried?"

"This is all new to me," she said. "I'm not a big fan of rituals and fantasy and mumbo jumbo, no offense, but this is not just about make believe. This is about bloody murder, and I guess it kind of got to me."

He rang for tea, and for the next hour they explored the ritual, he leafed back and forth through the book, explaining illustrations or peculiar words and spellings.

Kathy was fascinated with everything, from the musty odor to the whispery sound of pages as they turned. Some pages were more faded, leading her to wonder if the book had once been on display.

She picked up additional details. The parents of a maid who rejected a Stormont suitor, even if he had taken her life, were expected to furnish a written apology and absolve him of his 'crime of passion' to avoid ill will between families. *"Screw that!"* was her reaction to that, and Stormont laughed out loud.

As the iron gates of the estate swung closed behind her car, she felt a weight lift from her shoulders.

She rolled down the window and turned up the radio and felt grateful to be living in the 21st century. She thought about her next meeting with Sandy, he was a Goode Man. She chuckled to think that she had been frightened of the curse, then laughed to admit she was pleased that that same curse was promising her luck in love. Did she really believe in curses and blessings? *About as much as I believe in ghosts*, she thought ruefully. *In other words … maybe.*

36. Another Date With Madeline

Seated by the window in her apartment, wishing she had a garden, Kathy went over her notes. Rivers had given her an overview of how a Stormont man might react to rejection, but he hadn't been specific about holding the weapon to ensure a swift death. Deb and Grant had.

But he had said something odd at the end, quietly, almost to himself.

"So sad for such a beautiful object to be locked away. A beautiful woman lost, now a beautiful relic, rich in history, lost to the world, locked in an evidence box, gone forever." He sighed deeply. "Lost to the world, lost to us all." He had been arranging his pens and seemed to have forgotten she was there.

Kathy had been getting ready to leave. Ken Rivers had talked for a *long* time and she just wanted to get out of there. Now she mentally kicked herself for not following up on that comment. She wrote down his words exactly as she remembered them and underlined them.

...

As she dialed Madeline's number, she thought she would have to be *very* tactful to find out how her fingerprints happened to be on the dagger. She couldn't alarm her. She and Sandy had agreed they were not ready to reveal their evidence, but her fingerprints on the knife put Madeline at the top of their list of suspects. They had established possible motive, now they needed to know why she had touched the weapon – if it had not been to slay her sister.

Kathy half expected no answer from Madeline as it was mid-afternoon and she was pleased to hear her pick up.

She sounded tired. "Hello Kathy, how can I help now?"

"Hey Madeline, how are you doing?" She heard a sigh.

"Oh, alright. My husband's stable, showing some progress in therapy, so that's good. Work has been routine, no major accidents but I just finished a 14-hour shift. They did a double lung transplant, which was exciting." She laughed suddenly. "Actually, it exhilarating! But it's a long time to stand. My feet are killing me. Sorry, I'm rambling. What do you need?"

Kathy didn't want to keep her. "Are you coming to town anytime soon? I've got a couple more questions and I thought we might go somewhere nice, have coffee or lunch."

She heard a grunt and imagined Madeline kicking off her nurse's shoes and sitting down heavily. "Good timing," she said. "I'm in town tomorrow at the lawyers' about Shaye's will. I'm still stunned about it, but they're insistent and you were right, they *had* been trying to reach me. I have to listen to the will and get started on things, sign forms, be there in person."

Kathy hadn't expected such easy agreement. "That's great. What time will you be finished with the lawyers?"

"We meet at nine, so hopefully I'll be finished by 10?" Kathy made a doubtful noise, and Madeline chuckled. "Right, wishful thinking! Say 11 then. Meet after that?"

"Perfect!" said Kathy quickly. "Lunch it is. There's a Tim Horton's at the corner of your lawyer's building. We'll meet there. I'll come early, just in case you get done quickly."

Madeline was silent for a moment. "How do you know

where my lawyer's office is?"

Kathy grimaced. *Busted!* "Madeline you have to understand," she said reasonably. "I was the one who found Shaye. I'm involved in this whether I want to be or not. I found her, I called the cops. I've had to talk to the police, the coroner *and* the lawyers. There's an ongoing investigation," she spoke slowly, trying to recall what she had already told Madeline. "I'm done with the police now, but I'm also a journalist, remember." She was not sure she *had* told her that, but she ploughed on. "I'm writing a piece about this, not for sensation but to push for justice for Shaye and," she stopped herself before saying "the others."

Madeline was silent.

"Anyway," Kathy went on gamely. "The lawyers have access to part of the investigation. They had to confirm who had died, who is next of kin and all that stuff. So, yes, I know exactly where you're going to meet your lawyers. I'm on your side Madeline. I didn't mean to upset you." She grimaced again and held her breath, waiting to see how she would react. She heard another sigh. *She's probably rubbing her feet now.*

"I'm not upset. Just a little confused that you'd be involved with the lawyers but then I'm not used to this kind of thing. This whole thing is difficult. I was so happy to find my sister. Then she was taken away from me," a small, strangled noise came down the line. "Along with everything else going on, it's a bit bloody overwhelming."

"Hey, none of us are used to this kind of thing." *Except Sandy and that ice queen of a coroner* she was thinking. "Let's just keep our heads. I'll see you tomorrow around 11 at Tim Horton's at Chambers Lane and Center Street." She wanted to end on a high note. "It will be nice to see you again." She heard a little snort before Madeline said goodbye and hung up.

37. Maddy's Good Fortune

Kathy got to the cafe just after 10:30, although she had no illusions the meeting with her lawyers would be short. *Lawyers bill by the hour*, she thought as she slid into a booth.

She got comfortable, took out her laptop and notebook and waved cheerfully at the bored counter staff. She would wait for Madeline before ordering. If the counter kids had a problem with that, she'd go for a hot tea and a Timbit.

Madeline arrived just after 11, looking dazed. She sat down heavily. "Phew! It's good to see a familiar face. Have I kept you waiting? My head is reeling."

"I just got here," Kathy lied. "Relax, I'll order. Do you prefer tea or coffee? Want anything to eat?"

"I'll take a medium steeped tea with double milk no sugar," said Madeline with her eyes closed. "Please."

She opened her eyes and smiled. "I don't want anything to eat and I *never* say that! My stomach feels a little funny after all the hot air I was breathing up there."

Kathy gave Madeleines shoulder a gentle squeeze as she passed. She came back with the teas and two tea biscuits, in case Madeline changed her mind.

"Before we start on my questions, do you want to talk about it? You look kind of spaced out and I know a little about this legal stuff. I don't want to pry but if you want to talk to somebody, I'm here." She slurped her tea, and Madeline laughed.

"Spaced out is right. Thanks, I *would* like to talk a little.

You're probably going to find out everything anyway." She said it without rancor. She shrugged off her jacket, undid her top button and her rigid posture softened. She sipped her tea. Kathy waited patiently.

"I'm inheriting the house which is almost paid for, her car which is fully paid for, and a small investment portfolio that's more money than I've seen in my whole life," she said. "Six figures." She leaned forward. "That's what they said before they told me the actual amount, and I counted the zeroes in my head. I was *not* expecting that! I don't know what I'm going to do with it all."

That surprised Kathy, too. "So take it apart, think what you really need and what you've got here."

"Good plan," said Madeline, sipping her tea. "Just walking down here from the office I had some thoughts," she grinned. "Starting with the car, mine is nine years old with 300km on it, hers is not even a year old, a little red Santa Fe, so yes please! I can sell mine, it still goes alright and it doesn't owe me a thing. I'll sell it cheap to somebody who needs it."

"Right," said Kathy firmly. "No use driving around in an old car when you can have a new one for nothing, but wouldn't you keep the old one for your husband?"

Madeline looked even brighter. "I never thought about him driving again! It could happen. And there's room at the house for two cars."

Kathy thought about the old suburban bungalow, then saw again in her mind Shaye's pretty, urban cottage. She cleared her throat. "You'll sell Shaye's house, right?"

Madeline looked surprised. "Oh no. We're just renting where we are now. If we move into town we'll be closer to better therapy for my husband, and it's bigger, which will give us some room if we ever have kids." She stirred her tea thoughtfully. "It's not too far for me to drive to my work," her eyes were shining, "and I'll be driving against traffic with the hours I do."

A small bell went off in the back of Kathy's head. Some killers liked to return to the scene of the crime. Some took mementoes, a lock of hair, a book from the victim's home, others were drawn back to the location. It seemed odd for Madeline to want to set up home in the place where her sister had died.

"Do you think you'd feel okay living in that house, where Shaye died?"

Madeline shot her an odd, almost pitying look. "I'm a nurse, Kathy. I don't get spooked by death." Her face softened. "I get sad, of course, but we're a tough bunch, and I need to find some good in all this bad. Shaye is gone and I can't bring her back." She was silent for a moment. "Moving into the house feels like honoring her. As long as I have the house, she isn't completely gone."

Kathy lowered her head to hide a frown. *Honor again. It's starting to sound like a dangerous word.* She shook off the thought. *Focus on the fingerprints.* But before she started probing, she was happy to hear more about Madeline's plans.

Madeline intended to cash in some investments to pay for better therapy for her husband, and better lawyers, too.

"Our lawsuit against the company is getting nowhere, and the law firm handling it confuses me with all their legalese, they don't really try to explain. They're just condescending assholes," she said dismissively. "I can do better now."

"Sounds good," Kathy nodded her approval and then changed the subject.

38. Maddy's Dagger Fingerprints

Kathy had not spoken to Madeline about the Stormont dagger. Why would she? They had talked about Madeline's future, it was time to talk about the past. But what was the best way to start talking about the murder weapon, the rituals and the fact her fingerprints were on the knife that killed her sister? She would just begin and see how it went.

"Madeline," she began, glancing to her left and right to make it clear this was something sensitive. "As you know, I'm writing a piece about the Stormont dagger," she lowered her voice, "the murder weapon." Madeline nodded. "I'm writing with a historical perspective, because Shaye, God bless her, is the latest in a long line of women who've been involved with the dagger over generations."

Madeline was watching her closely. Kathy ploughed on. "Have you ever seen it?"

"Seen what?"

"The dagger. The Stormont dagger. Have you ever seen it?"

Madeline gazed levelly at her. "Why do you ask?"

She hadn't answered the question. Kathy saw traces of the tense, hostile person she had met at their first interview. She had struck a nerve.

Be careful, she thought. She couldn't say police had Madeline's fingerprints on the knife, because the police didn't know that – not officially.

"It's been in the papers and on TV, you must have seen it. I just wondered how much you know about its history and," she shrugged, "whether you'd ever run into it before. I'd never heard of it, but you'd be surprised how many people *are* familiar with the whole story."

Madeline raised an eyebrow, leaned back, relaxed her shoulders. She seemed to come to a decision. ,

"Off the record? I'll tell you this as a friend, I don't want it spread around. Agreed?" Kathy opened her mouth to remind her new friend that she was a journalist, but she closed it again.

Madeline was tense but ready to confide in her. If she stayed calm, she might hear something critical to the case. If she made a wrong move, Madeline could shut down.

"You have my word. Two friends talking, just between you and me."

Madeline sighed. "I'm sorry for the attitude, but I'm less trusting since the accident. Money's tight. I'm trying to hang on to our rental house. His medications are expensive and the lousy, lying company is doing everything it can not to cover them."

She stopped and collected herself.

"Recently I took a side job with a catering company. I got my SmartServe bartending licence when I put myself through nursing school. I did a lot of events back then, but I hadn't done it for a long time. It was Shaye who introduced me to the catering company. She figured it was extra money and would get me out of the house, give me something else to think about." She smiled, remembering.

"We did a couple of lunchtime things. It wasn't hard, it was fun and Shaye liked meeting new people, especially interesting men. Then we did a gala for the Stormont family, one of their charity events at that big house."

***

Kathy clenched her fists under the table.

"Before the party started, Mr. Stormont gathered the hired help by the fireplace to see his famous dagger. He opened up an old box and took out some ratty old gloves and this big fancy knife and told us about its history. Then he let us hold it. Well, some of us held it. He wanted us to get a sense of the history in his family so we could answer questions if any guests asked. I remember thinking, hey I'm only getting thirteen bucks an hour for this, I don't think so.

"This friend of Mr. Stormont's, a teacher called Dr. Rivers had arrived early and he joined in to offer his own expertise. He seemed to think it was a waste of time telling the stories to *waitresses*, and said we should send guests with questions to him. He was kind of full of himself, but Shaye was talking to him, flirting really, during the party. I had to give her a nudge to keep her moving with the drinks." She stopped and slumped a little.

"Maddy, what is it?" Kathy said softly.

"I feel like shit talking about it. There we were oohing and ahh-ing over some stupid old knife to be polite to a client," tears welled up, "when it was a ~~fucking~~ murder weapon!"

Kathy took her hand. "I'm so sorry. I didn't want to cause you pain. I hadn't really thought how you must feel about it. I'm truly sorry."

"That's okay," she said, wiping at her tears. "I didn't realize how emotional I'd get talking about it."

Kathy was puzzled. Madeline blew hot and cold. She had legitimate reasons to be emotional and also wary and locked down. But Kathy had studied killers and knew that some could detach themselves from what they had done, be genuinely heartbroken over the loss of a loved one and 'forget' they were responsible for the killing.

Madeline had recovered her composure. "Do you have any other questions? That's really all I know about the dagger, or the Stormont family, and I don't want to know any more. I just want to know who killed my sister."

"No more questions, and I have to go. Thanks for being honest with me, I'm sorry it got rough." Madeline waved that away.

They had a hug before going opposite ways. Madeline had to hurry to catch a train, Kathy was happy to walk the mile and a half home and think about things.

She had a plausible explanation for Madeline's prints on the dagger. She still didn't know for sure if Madeline had known about Shaye's wealth and her will. She liked Maddy, but she was still on their list of suspects – in fact pretty close to the top.

39. Breakfast Debrief

Detective Brampton opened his car door and felt the summer heat rush in. One of the perks of being a Detective Sergeant was the air-conditioned car, and feeling that blast of hot air reminded him how far he'd come from his foot patrol and traffic duty days.

Another perk was freedom to get out of the station any time of day. Breakfast at Rosy's was a great way to start the day, a good place to sit and think. The squad room would be alive with energy, phones ringing, people asking questions and well-meaning colleagues interrupting him every few minutes. He wanted time alone, but he was also hoping Kathy would show up to report on her meeting with Madeline.

He'd barely settled into their usual booth when Lucy appeared at his elbow.

"Hello, detective," she said, drawing out the first word. "Is it a coffee morning or a tea morning?" If he said coffee she knew he'd eat, drink and run. If he ordered a pot of tea, he'd spend some time sitting and thinking. Lucy prided herself on understanding her regulars.

"Definitely a tea morning, thank you Lucy."

When Kathy walked in Brampton felt a rush of pleasure. She wore a plain beige linen dress that ended just above her knees. Her legs were smooth and brown, her sandals were low and comfortable and a well-tailored jacket made it all look professional.

"Hello Sandy. Ready for the next round?"

"Ready when you are partner."

She slid into her seat, smiling at being called partner. "I saw Madeline yesterday and we've got something."

Lucy had been standing by the table and when Kathy paused she jumped in. "Tea for you too, Kathy?"

"Yes, please Lucy. I'm starving, but I need to think about what I want. I see Sandy's got a big pot, but he'll be needing it all for himself." He didn't argue. "So just a cup of tea for me to start."

Lucy bobbed a little curtsy and turned back to the kitchen.

"So, what did you find out? Do we know how her prints got on the dagger?"

"Yep," said Kathy, and held his eyes. He waited then made an exasperated noise. "Please do go on," he said with exaggerated politeness.

"I got it, but I don't know how much it helps."

She told him about the sisters doing catering gigs, and when she got to the part about working at the Stormont Estate his eyebrows shot up.

"It gets weirder," she said. "Gordon thought it was a good idea to show the catering staff some of his treasures including the dagger. Rivers was there too. I get the impression he never misses an opportunity to show off and he joined in. Stormont was giving the girls a sort of primer in case guests asked them about Stormont history." Brampton looked skeptical and she tipped her head in acknowledgement. "I know, they're there to serve drinks and he's coaching them on family's history, but he invited them to hold it, which explains Maddy's prints on the knife, along with a few others. She says some of them shrank away but she's not easily spooked. Blades don't bother her. Afterall she is a surgical nurse and sees flesh cut all the time. It sounds plausible to me."

Brampton considered, then said, "There's a clear print from Madeline's thumb near the hilt. If she'd used it to stab someone, her prints would be on the handle."

"I'm not ready to rule her out," Kathy said stubbornly.

Lucy arrived with the tea. "Any decisions yet about breakfasts?"

"Oatmeal for me with brown sugar." Brampton seemed bent on avoiding bacon.

"Brown toast with blueberry jam for me, thanks, and better put some fruit on his oatmeal Lucy, we don't want him getting scurvy." Kathy sipped her tea gratefully and continued her report. Sandy just smiled at her ordering for him.

"Madeline's getting Shaye's house and plans to live there. I don't know how happy she'll be. It wouldn't suit me to live in a place where somebody I love was murdered, but she wants to keep the good memories of times she shared there with her sister."

Brampton shrugged. "Lot of people preserve a room just as the victim left it. If she can hold onto happy memories and not be bothered by bad ones, that's her call. Anything else?"

She told him about Ashbury's photographs, the girls, the beach shots and the startling news that he'd photographed Catrina Somers before her death.

"He's bringing me his collections next week."

Brampton wondered what she expected to find.

"I won't know until I see it, but I have a feeling." Her famous *spidey sense*, he thought. It made him smile. She saw it and said defiantly, "It would be remiss to *not* look at pictures someone has of *two* dead women! And he's got pictures of Channel Lane Point. Those were Shaye's dying words."

40. Autopsies And Curses

Brampton was satisfied. "Okay my turn. Catrina's autopsy. There were marks on the back of her neck consistent with her being held, like someone held all her dead weight," he grimaced. "Sorry, bad choice of words. Not exactly fingerprints, but consistent with a hand or palm of a hand.."

"Gloves," exclaimed Kathy. "Those deerskin gloves wouldn't leave fingerprints but they could leave a mark. Check with Linda to see if that's possible."

"I'll call her, and we can get a fuller description of the missing gloves from Gordon."

Lucy placed their breakfasts in front of them, nudging the blueberries close to Brampton. He reached over them for the brown sugar and dumped two large spoonfuls onto his oatmeal followed by five berries.

"What about Deborah. Did she have much to add to our understanding of the ceremony?"

"She was excited to talk about it. She's obsessed with the pedigree and history of the dagger, but disgusted by the misogyny of it all. By my count we still have three suspects, and no reason to rule any of them out."

Brampton agreed. "Three with motive and a connection to the dagger. The only one who didn't benefit from Shaye's death is Ashbury, but for him it could have been a crime of passion."

Kathy disliked that expression, but she nodded. "I'll talk to Grant when he brings me his photographs, you keep digging into Deb's background and Maddy's finances." She sipped her tea and decided to share what she'd learned about the Stormont curse. "Want to hear some good news?"

"I'm always up for good news," he smiled. "Don't often get it."

"Gordon Stormont showed me the famous book where all the information about the dagger and the rituals are written down. It's beautiful, gold leaf edges, illustrations, the whole nine yards." She took a sip and waited for him to ask for more.

"Is this about the curse? We already know bad luck strikes anyone who doesn't do the mumbo jumbo right. Are you telling me there's a chapter on women who find women who've been stabbed by Stormont men?" He was laughing, and Kathy bristled.

"As a matter of fact there is. I guess I'm not the only one to hold a victim of the dagger as she died. I don't *really* believe in this kind of thing, but I was a little concerned to think I'd got involved with a bloody curse. Anyway, the short answer is I'm going to be rewarded with good luck for all my days," she shuddered. "Horrible way to earn it."

Brampton felt sorry for mocking. "Come on Kathy, there's more to it than that, I'm sure. What's the full version?"

"I thought it was strange they would even cover the eventuality, but the whole thing is strange. The book says if I somehow ended up holding a woman who was stabbed as part of the ritual, and if I held her right, I will supposedly be lucky in love. I'll find my forever love and we'll have children and they'll be blessed forever and ever amen. Lucky bloody me."

She lowered her head to hide the tears springing to her eyes and missed his startled expression and something that flashed in his eyes. But she felt the warmth of his hand as he placed it over hers.

"Lucky in love, eh? That's not a bad thing. Maybe we can find a silver lining after all, take advantage of being on the right side of a curse, eh?"

She looked up quickly. He said maybe *we* can find a silver lining. Is he joking? She looked into his blue eyes and thought *no he's not.*

41. Handing Over Pictures

Ashbury was waiting for her at the security desk of her office building. He was holding two bankers' boxes and looking strained. When he'd said *a couple* she thought it would be two albums, not two big boxes.

"Wow, that's a lot of photographs, Grant."

"I haven't looked at them in a while," he said breathlessly, dropping them onto the desk. "I remembered storing albums in the basement, but when I saw how many there were, I thought what a chore it will be for you to go through them all." He patted the closest box. "They're probably of no interest to anyone but me, but if they help catch a killer I'm glad to share."

He paused, waiting for her to say something grateful. When she missed her cue, he shrugged and turned to smile at the camera that would spit out his visitor's badge.

With the badge clipped to his shirt, he lifted the boxes with a grunt and walked through the security arch with Kathy following.

"Give me one of those," she reached for the top box.

"It's okay, they're not that heavy."

"Come on, it's the 21st century, women share the load." She grabbed the box and found it much heavier than expected, she staggered but smiled, glad that she'd kept up the weight training with Deborah.

They rode the elevator in silence up to the third floor, walked down the corridor to a small meeting room where she dropped her box onto a table and tapped two buttons on a console built into its polished surface. Overhead lights came on and translucent shades slid smoothly down over the glass walls and door making the room totally private.

Ashbury put down his box and eased into a high-backed leather chair. "Where shall we start?"

"Take it from the top," she said lightly. "Start with the first album and work our way through."

She pulled a chair up beside him and began leafing through the first album. The first thing she saw was he had a good eye for composition and lighting.

"These are good. Have you thought of showing them?"

He looked pleased. "I never got around to it, then digital photography took over and everything was being shared on social media. I stopped printing and kind of forgot about my old work."

"Shame." She meant it. "You have a good style. Did you enter any contests?"

"Interesting you should ask. Four years ago I sent a print to a local juried show and won second prize," he said. "But it was only ever a hobby. I thought I was good, but not many people saw my work, so I didn't really know."

Kathy flipped to the end then took out a second album. This was going to take longer than she had time for today. She wanted to study them, not just glance through and make encouraging noises.

"I didn't expect so many photos, can I take them home? Rather than take up your time, I'll go through them over the weekend and get them back to you Monday." She leaned forward and said in a conspiratorial tone, "I promise nobody else will see them."

Ashbury hesitated, then smiled. "Keep them as long as you want. I haven't looked at them in years and can't remember what's here, but if they might hold clues, go for it." He flipped the second album shut. "What are we looking for?"

Kathy ignored the we. She tucked the two albums back into the box and fitted the cardboard lid before answering.

"I don't know. It's all part of investigative reporting, you don't know what you're looking for until you find it. A line of enquiry can be a complete dead end or spark a new idea that really does go somewhere."

He seemed satisfied with that, and they walked in amiable silence down the hall and rode the elevator down. They carried one box each to Kathy's car and she used her foot to open the trunk, impressing Ashbury with her agility which was increasing, thanks to Deborah, the oddball new friend and murder suspect.

As she drove off, Kathy could see Grant Ashbury watching her until she turned a corner and went out of sight.

42. Catrina Naked

Saturday morning Kathy made a large pot of tea, shook three oatmeal cookies onto a plate, then reconsidered and took the whole packet to the table where the boxes of photos awaited. She was going to need sustenance to go through all those pictures.

Two hours later she had looked through six albums in the first box and eaten seven cookies. Nothing jumped out, but something nagged her, and she felt sure something was there, hiding in plain view. It hadn't been in the first box. She resisted reaching for another cookie, just licked her finger to dab at crumbs on the plate.

The first box had contained a lot of girls in bathing suits and short shorts. She reminded herself Grant had taken them as a young university student. As she moved along the timeline the pictures became more artistic, less voyeuristic, fewer girls, more empty landscapes. By the time she finished the first box she was starting to miss the bathing beauties.

In the second box she found more landscapes, more beach shots, a few portraits. She went slowly, looking for anything unusual, or – conversely – any*body* familiar.

She felt a trickle of excitement when she opened the penultimate album in the second box and saw pictures of a pretty cottage. Grant had shot it from the front and back, from a distance and close up. There were details of the windows, even one of the roof tiles. *I'd have thrown that one out,* she thought, then shook herself and thought, *don't be bitchy.* She sighed and set the album to one side. It could be important.

The first page of the last album was an empty beach, the second page was a shock. It held a single photo, a headshot of a beautiful girl laughing and tossing her hair. Underneath it, in neat black handwriting, it said Catrina Somers. Kathy was looking at the cold case murder victim. She really was lovely with flawless skin, large dark eyes and perfect white teeth.

The third page held another surprise, Catrina in the nude. It was subtle, her arm placed demurely across her breasts, one long leg drawn up and face turned slightly away. Her eyes were downcast, but, having seen her face on the previous page, there was no doubt it was Catrina.

The next page had three smaller prints of Catrina on the beach in a bathing suit. In two of them she was looking straight at the camera in the third she looked out over the water.

The following pages had long shots of Catrina on the beach. Kathy guessed they were taken with a long lens and Catrina seemed unaware of being photographed.

The surprises kept coming. There was a shot taken from outside the cottage, looking through the window. It was artsy, roses framing the window were softly blurred, but the figure in the room was in perfect focus. Catrina, naked, toweling her wet hair, not looking toward the camera.

Kathy held her breath as she turned the page to find a naked woman in the arms of a fully clothed man. They were kissing. The picture was not sharp, it was taken through a window and Kathy wondered how far away Grant had been. She was sure it was Catrina, but she couldn't see the man's face, only long fair hair, a pale shirt and trousers and blurry hands, one on the small of her back, the other gripping her neck. She peered at the image, cursing the poor quality.

Kathy took a swig of cold tea, grimaced and pushed the last album aside. She went back to the previous album, to the pictures of the cottage. It was the same building.

Who owned it? Why was Catrina there? And who was she kissing? It wasn't Grant, because Grant had been taking the pictures.

43. Who Owns The Cottage?

The Land Registry Office was open until 1 o'clock on Saturdays. It was 12:15 when Kathy called the direct line for Estelle Canton. Her friend worked reception on a Saturday because her husband Ed was home to mind the girls, and because it paid time and a half. "Compton Land Registry, Estelle speaking, how can I help you," she answered in a cheery singsong voice.

"Estelle! It's Kathy, how *are* you, and how are the kids?" Estelle laughed. She knew Kathy was after a favor. They had been friends for years, and Kathy had given her encouragement and support at least as many times as she'd given Kathy inside information.

"Jenny's going into grade 8 and wants to go on the pill. Peter graduated grade 9 and wants to be a scientist. He's got the grades, but Ed wants him to join his accounting business. Jonathon is still a handful and he's going into grade 6 in September if I don't kill him first and bury him in the garden. How's you?"

She was rewarded with a laugh. "I'm great, but listen, can you tell me who owns a certain cottage out at the point?"

"If you tell me which one you mean, I can tell you in about ten seconds. Address?" Estelle never questioned why Kathy needed to know.

"Hmm, I'm not sure, but it's the last cottage before you get onto the beach, before the timber archway on the east side."

Kathy could hear Estelle on the keyboard. She waited patiently.

"Got it. It's called Rose Cottage, one of the originals, built in 1908 by John James Rivers. It's been in the family ever since and the current owner is," tap, tap, "Dr. Ken Rivers."

Kathy blinked and said nothing for a good five seconds. "Did you say Ken Rivers?"

"Yes, it was transferred to him 16 years ago as part of the previous owner's estate."

Kathy fought down her excitement. "Estelle, honey, thanks so much. I owe you a coffee. How about Thursday? I can catch up on that crazy family of yours."

Estelle's laugh came out like a bark. "It's a date, but let's not talk about my gang, you can tell me what you've been up to. Like, have you asked that detective fella out yet? Clock's ticking, girl."

"You old mother hen! There's not much to tell." She heard Estelle snort. "But let's do it, see you at Tim's next Thursday. Is nine-thirty too early?"

Estelle chuckled. "The kids are old enough to pour their own damned cereal. I'll be there."

Kathy disconnected and sat quietly. Had Catrina been more than just a student to the preening Dr. Ken? What was she doing in his cottage, and were those his hands on her slender naked back?

44. Maddy At The Station

Brampton met Madeline Saunders at the front desk of the police station and escorted her to an interrogation room. They exchanged pleasantries as they walked, nobody took any notice as they passed through offices and corridors, and Madeline felt more relaxed by the time they reached Interrogation Room D than she had since leaving home.

He motioned her to a chair on one side of the desk and sat down in one of the two chairs opposite. He placed a brown folder on the table. She glanced briefly at it before turning to look around the room noting the small camera high on one wall and the large mirror on another. She stared at the mirror, patted her hair and raised her eyebrows for the benefit of anyone watching.

Brampton noticed the gesture. *Damned cop shows* he thought, but said, "I've asked Kathy to join us if that's okay with you?"

"Fine with me," said Madeline. She had no idea why she was there, even less of a clue why Kathy Chatsworth would join them, but she would stay calm and see what unfolded.

Two minutes later, the door opened and Kathy stepped in. She greeted Madeline, gave her a brief hug before taking the seat next to Brampton.

He cleared his throat and began. "Part of why we're here today is to sign the form to release Shaye's house from police custody to you. I'm recording the meeting to help me make my notes and serve as future reference for you if your lawyers need it."

"This is partly to release my house, but there's more to it? Is that what you're saying?" Madeline looked from Brampton to Kathy.

"Mrs. Saunders, we have some questions to ask as part of our investigation," he'd meant to call her Madeline but old habits are hard to break. "Are you comfortable answering questions today?"

Madeline turned to stare at the mirror and laughed. "My goodness, shouldn't I have a lawyer present?" Brampton opened his mouth to reply, but she waved her hand dismissively. "I'm kidding. Go ahead. If I start feeling uncomfortable, I can just stop right?" He nodded warily. "But if I stop before you're satisfied, I might not get my house released today?"

He silently swore at the cop shows again and repeated, "We're here to release your house, but we also have some questions."

Madeline took pity on him. "Okay detective, fire away."

He pressed record. "This is Detective Sergeant Brampton," he emphasized the title, "interviewing Madeline Saunders with Kathy Chatsworth as witness. We'll be discussing items regarding the Shaye Alderson murder investigation. Madeline, please confirm you are aware this is being recorded."

She leaned forward and spoke clearly into the small recording machine. "Madeline Saunders speaking. Yes, I'm aware this is being recorded and I fully agree to it. I do not have counsel present, nor do I believe I need it."

He dated and timed the recording and moved to his first question.

"Madeline, I understand you have family issues that have put you in debt. With the death of Shaye Alderson, you have inherited her estate, which will solve that problem. Help me understand your perspective on this."

Madeline listened intently, then genuine surprise lit up her face and she laughed out loud and reached under the desk.

"I'm reaching into my briefcase now for my iPad," she said, perhaps confusing the interrogation with a late-night traffic stop. Kathy stifled a giggle, Brampton looked annoyed. "Because it will help with this conversation," Madeline said clearly. She activated PowerPoint.

"If you'd just asked me about this, I could have made it really simple." She spun the iPad around to face them. "Shaye was going to loan me money. She wanted to give it to me, but I insisted I would pay it back, so we agreed on a loan with very low interest."

Kathy was surprised. This had not come up in their lengthy conversations. Brampton had on his poker face and just nodded.

"Shaye wanted to use the law firm of Jackson, Jackson and Kelsey, who I think you're familiar with?" Madeline asked.

"Yes, I'm familiar with them," said Brampton stiffly.

"They're the lawyers I use for my family business," said Kathy helpfully.

Madeline turned her device around and typed rapidly, then turned it back.

"Here is the promissory note drafted by that firm." She touched the screen making a soft indent. "It's dated the day before she died. You're welcome to read it. You'll see there's a onetime interest payment. It says I can pay back the loan any time within five years. You'll see I was setting up a trust account with them so I could make payments whenever I had money available."

Brampton picked up the iPad, scanned the document, then placed it back on the desktop and nodded for her to continue.

"So you see, money was no longer an issue. Thanks to Shaye I was going to have access to what I needed when I needed it."

They sat in silence and, before they could respond, Madeline sat back with a tight smile on her face.

"I do understand. When I showed up just after her murder, I was an obvious suspect – a mysterious, long-lost sister in financial trouble." Kathy heard the hurt in her voice. "You *actually* thought I could have murdered her. I was coming to the city the day after she died so we could finalize how to set up this money."

She looked suddenly tired, reminding Kathy that her life was not easy. "We were going to go shopping," Madeline said softly. "We liked shopping together."

Sandy moved the iPad back to her. "I wish we had known all this before. You're right, it takes away what would have been a strong motive."

45. Love Child

"Thanks Madeline," said Kathy. "We understand about the money now, but I'm not sure I understand why you would want to keep the house after what happened there."

Madeline cast her eyes down, gathering her thoughts, or thinking up a lie, Kathy thought cynically.

"Let me tell you about that house," she said after a long silence. "You're recording this but I'd ask you to please not share what I'm going to tell you, unless it's absolutely necessary."

She had their attention.

"My biological father bought the house before he was married. He lived his whole life there, and he lived there with his wife," she paused and looked at the mirror, "his wife who was not my mother." They nodded. "His wife was not a gardener, but my father loved his garden." Kathy felt a pang of sympathy for this woman who had never met her dad but clung to the little she knew about him. "Shaye and her dad, that is my dad, I mean her dad," Madeline's voice broke, "he and Shaye worked together in the garden. She told me all about it and said it was some of the happiest times she could recall." She glanced at the mirror, met her own eyes and turned away.

"When Shaye was seven, she and her mom went to visit an aunt in Vancouver for most of the summer, leaving her dad alone. That was the summer he met my mother.

"I told Kathy how they met at a conference. He was on his own for weeks that summer and they saw each other for walks and drinks and who knows what else. Inevitably he invited her to the house. I don't think I told Kathy that before."

Kathy had wondered then just how much Madeline knew about her mother's affair. She was about to find out.

Madeline continued recklessly, "They made love in the garden, in the pool, in the porch swing. My mother said she refused to do it in his bed or anywhere inside the house." Just as suddenly as she had started, she stopped.

"Go on," said Brampton softly.

"She got pregnant," said Madeline forcefully. "She knew he'd offer to support her, and she knew it would be horrible for his wife if she found out. She felt guilty and knew she wouldn't carry on the affair when his family came home. She told me she loved him, but she let him go."

It was very quiet in Interrogation Room D. Kathy held her breath. Brampton wondered where this story was going.

"She'd been looking to leave Toronto and her high pressure hospital, even before she met him," Madeline continued. "They were crying out for surgical nurses in Kingston, five hours away. There was no future in Toronto, she didn't want to break up his family, so she left. She pretty much ran away at the end of August and never told him where she was going. He never knew she was pregnant. He never knew he had another daughter."

Madeline's eyes glistened but she held her head up, daring them to say something. Nobody spoke, and her shoulders slumped a little.

"Our dad was only the second owner of the house, Shaye was the third, and I will be the fourth, so it's staying in our dad's bloodline. I never knew him, but I knew Shaye, and she shared her memories with me of living there and working in the garden." She laughed suddenly. "Chances are I was conceived in the garden, so I'm like a flower he planted. His flower child."

46. I'm Not Signing Anything

Kathy looked at Brampton for guidance on how to respond. She got nothing. "I think you're brave for sharing all this," she said cautiously. "And you're brave to take on the house, I think your dad and your sister would be pleased," she spoke sincerely, but finished with a frown which Madeline picked up on.

"There's a but?" she asked.

"You're very open today," Kathy said, "we appreciate that, but when I spoke to you before, you often seemed anxious and guarded. There were times I wondered if you were being totally honest with me."

Madeline wasn't offended. "Let me put this in perspective. I'm a surgical nurse which can be traumatic. My husband has had a dreadful accident, and unless we spend a lot of time and money he may never work again. I'm fighting a heartless company for compensation. Did I tell you they brought five lawyers to our first meeting and about a hundred pages for me to sign? I couldn't understand them so I didn't sign them. Then you come snooping around, for all I know you're working for that company or undercover for the police because, oh yes, my sister was murdered by some ceremonial fanatic." She tipped her head. "Yes, I was a little tense."

Kathy decided to plough on. She still had questions. "You told me a different story about your mom and Shaye's dad, you said it was just a brief encounter. It was a lot more than that."

Madeline opened her mouth and shut it again. She drew a big breath. "Okay. What I told you at first was the story my mother told me. This one is the true story, the one I heard from Shaye, and she knew it because her dad confided in her before he died. He never knew about the pregnancy, he just told her that he'd been in love with another woman who had gone away and broken his heart. He begged her not to tell her mother. Shaye never told anyone but me – why would she? I had no idea the story would be of interest to you, Kathy, so I told you my mom's version."

At this point, Brampton seemed to wake from his reverie. "Tell me about this issue with your husband."

"What do you want to know?" she sighed. "You could get all the information you need from the company or the lawyers."

Brampton was unfazed. "It sounds like you need a hand. I don't know if I can help, but maybe Jackson, Jackson and Kelsey can."

She considered. "The company says John was drunk. If he was drunk, he'd be responsible for the accident and they'd be off the hook." She shifted in her chair and looked uncomfortable. "The day of the accident there had been a small party in the back of the warehouse where beer and liquor were being served and John had stopped in for a few minutes before his shift. They jumped on the chance to claim he was drunk."

Kathy asked gently, "Madeline, is it possible he had been drinking?"

"No!" Madeline said loudly. "My husband does not drink. I've said it and said it again, but they don't want to hear it. He's had maybe three drinks in all the time I've known him, and that was including a glass of wine one Christmas that his bloody brother practically poured down his throat. He doesn't like the taste, he doesn't like the sensation, so he just doesn't bother with booze. If people get insistent he tells them it would be a waste of alcohol because he's tried it and he doesn't like it. That usually puts them off. Our friends and his workmates know he only drinks soft drinks and wouldn't even bother to offer him alcohol."

"Why didn't the company just ask his workmates?" Kathy asked.

Madeline shrugged. "It's not what they want to hear. The real issue is the equipment he was using had no safety guard and the company had been cited several times for not following regulations. The machine requires constant maintenance and with the safety guard in place they have to shut down the whole line to do maintenance. Without it they can just slow down the line to do a fix. Everybody knows it's not safe, but they do it. If the company is found guilty of endangering the workers, ignoring regulations, there will be a huge government fine."

Kathy began to see the big picture. It was worth paying a team of expensive lawyers to fight the little nurse and her injured husband. Brampton seemed satisfied with her explanation.

"Okay, let's move on to the house release. It's a seven-page legal form we need you to sign."

She sat back and folded her arms across her chest. "I want my lawyers to look at it before I sign anything," Madeline said.

"It really is just a standard form," he said patiently. "I'm not trying to put anything over on you."

"Detective Brampton, my lawyer specifically told me

not to sign *anything* until he's looked at it."

47. Bring In The Big Guns

Brampton sat back, echoing her posture. The two women watched him. Finally he spoke. "Madeline, have you heard of the senior at Jackson Jackson and Kesley, Charles Montgomery Peter Jackson?"

"Absolutely. I deal with Jeb Stone, but I have met Charles Jackson senior, and Charles Jackson junior. Jackson Senior has been generous with his time, giving advice on our case." That didn't surprise Brampton. Jackson Senior had more money than God and was interested in David and Goliath cases.

"I think we can find a solution. May I call Charles on your behalf?"

She agreed.

"Hello Mr. Jackson," he said loudly into the phone. "No golf today? Yes, yes, of course I remember you beat me by one stroke at the charity game and, no, I'm not paying you ten bucks. No, Chuck, listen to me. I paid it, check your pockets." Kathy rolled her eyes at Madeline. "I'm here with Madeline Saunders and we want to release her house to her but you guys have taught her well. She's not signing anything without you or Jeb's input. I'll put you on speaker phone."

He touched the speakerphone connection, then nodded encouragingly at Madeline who leaned close to the phone. "Hello Mr. Jackson."

"Hello Madeline, how are you doing my dear?"

"Pretty good, considering," she replied. "They're recording this so you have to speak up."

The elderly man chuckled. "Yes, ma'am." He adopted a booming, courtroom voice. "For the record I am Charles Montgomery Peter Jackson, and I am a representative of Madeline Saunders for her legal matters."

Madeline nodded and Kathy gave her a thumbs up.

"I have standard property release form 107-8566 in front of me on my screen, Sandy, I assume it's the 09/17 version?" Jackson Senior walked them through each paragraph of the document, translating complex language where necessary. Before turning a page, he asked Madeline to confirm her understanding of what she had read and sign at the bottom right. Each time, Kathy signed on the left as a witness.

After fifteen minutes they were done.

"Thank you so much, Mr. Jackson," Madeline said, "what do I owe you?"

A soft chuckle came from the speaker. "That will be $100 please. Not our standard fee, but it's also not that silly TV stuff where you give me a dollar and I take your case. If you could get Bampton to cough up ten bucks I'll drop it to ninety."

Madeline was satisfied. Brampton clipped the pages together, they said their goodbyes to the speakerphone, then sat for a moment in silence.

Brampton was first to speak, for the benefit of the recording machine.

"This concludes the discussion with Madeline Saunders, Kathy Chatsworth, and Detective Sergeant Sandy Brampton in the Shaye Alderson case. It included signing of legal documents to release property being held in evidence to Mrs. Saunders." He hit the button and they all exhaled, as if they'd been holding their breath for an hour.

"Just relax here and I'll walk this down to the clerk." He pushed his chair back, stood and stretched his legs. He understood the psychology hard chairs in interrogation rooms, but he didn't like it. "They can process it right away and provide the release document. We can email a copy to your lawyers and you can have the original." He smiled then, "along with the house keys. Won't be long."

Madeline looked like she was going to cry, and Kathy thought back to their meeting at the cafe when she was dazed after meeting with lawyers. There was something numbing about the archaic language used in legal documents.

"Works for me," said Madeline. "My neighbour is sitting with John, and I wanted to stay in town long enough to get into the house, water the plants, let in some fresh air. Now I can do it without a policeman watching me."

Brampton took the folder and left the room. Kathy stood and stretched her arms above her head with a little sigh. "This took longer than we expected, can I get you a coffee, tea, glass of water?" She could have murdered a glass of wine.

"Water, thank you," Madeline said sweetly.

With two paper cups of water in front of them, they made small talk for ten minutes. Madeline made it clear she didn't want to talk about her husband's lawsuit and when they fell silent for a minute or two it felt fine. Only the chairs were uncomfortable.

Brampton returned with the envelope and keys with a large red evidence tag attached.

"This is the release form. You can't move in until probate of the will is finalized, but you're free to visit the house on your own," he handed everything to her. "No policemen."

Now the tears began to flow and Madeline wiped them with her sleeve before Kathy could hand her a tissue.

She dabbed her eyes then suddenly stood. "Right! That's one thing resolved." No-nonsense Madeline was back.

"Make that two things," Kathy smiled and looked at Brampton enquiringly. He placed his hand on Madeline's shoulder.

"Maddy, you are no longer a suspect in the murder of Shaye Alderson," he said.

"My sister," Madeline said, fixing him with a steely look.

"Your sister," he agreed.

48. Deb's A Liar – In A Good Way

Kathy struggled into Brampton's office with the two white banker's boxes filled with photo albums. She expected him to rush to her aid, but as soon as she appeared he grabbed a large brown envelope from his desk and headed for the door.

"Just put them down on the side table, Kathy. We're going to interrogation room B to talk to Deborah."

Before Kathy could ask questions, he was gone. She glanced doubtfully at the small table then dropped the boxes on the floor and hurried after him.

In the interrogation room Deborah sat calmly at the table. The room was identical to the one they had spent the previous afternoon in with Madeline. Kathy sighed as she took her seat on the other side of the table but gave herself a shake and resolved to do her best to help Brampton.

"Thank you for coming in today Deborah I just have a few questions, I think we can clear up this whole situation and, hopefully, remove you from our suspect list," he said.

"That would be wonderful," said Deborah cheerily. "Because I didn't kill her."

Brampton placed the envelope in front of her, tapped it with a finger and asked a question that would change the case forever. "Who are the Hopkins Sisters, Deborah?"

She blinked rapidly, she looked surprised. "Those

women who write a home decorating column?"

Brampton held her eyes and said, "I'll repeat that. *Who are* the Hopkins Sisters? Not what do they do for a living."

She didn't respond, only stared back, then glanced over at Kathy, then looked down at her hands. "Well I don't know *who* the Hopkins sisters are. I don't think anybody knows, because they don't go on talk shows or anything," she turned to Kathy with a *help me* look.

Brampton picked up the envelope and slapped it down, making them jump.

"Yesterday, one of the Hopkins Sisters picked up an envelope from a post office box. The envelope was from the editor of the Dallas Lone Star newspaper that published their first column and today controls its syndication. The letter was asking them to write a column about paint colours for autumn and to think about one on Victorian chairs. The editor is a lousy speller, he had chairs spelled with two R's."

Deborah started as if she'd had an electric shock. She recovered her composure and shrugged. "What's this got to do with me?"

"There may be a photograph in this envelope," he picked it up and waved it at her. "If I open it we might see an image of a woman about your height opening that post office box and removing a letter addressed to the Hopkins Sisters. If that is the case this has a *lot* to do with you."

Deborah put her head in her hands. "Oh shit, you know, don't you," she said.

"I know some of it," said Brampton, not unkindly. "I'm interested in your side of the story."

Kathy looked from one to the other, trying to keep up. "Are *you* one of the Hopkins sisters?" she asked. When Deborah didn't answer, she said hesitantly, "Who's the other one?"

Deborah raised her head, she was fighting tears and losing the battle.

"The other Hopkins sister is, I mean was, Shaye Alderson."

49. Deb's Secret

Kathy was astonished. Hadn't Deb despised and resented Shaye? Isn't that why they were investigating her? Brampton was still treating her as a suspect, so there must be something else going on, some other motive to kill. She turned to him, but he gestured for her to keep quiet.

"Tell me about your real relationship with Shaye," he said.

"It started when she was at the ad agency doing copywriting," Deborah began. "She'd only been there a couple of weeks when we had a summer picnic party. She looked lost, sitting on her own, so I went over to chat. We talked about writing and our ambitions, and then we talked about our apartments and it turned out we are both really into decorating." Kathy noticed the slip back into the present tense.

"Shaye had written stuff for a home decor blog, and I was a huge fan of those things, so we got carried away with the idea of pitching a column, writing it together under a pseudonym. That way if it bombed it wouldn't hurt our careers, and we could be a bit daring with it. We just wanted to have fun."

"It seems to have worked out," said Brampton dryly. "It went into syndication, didn't it?"

Deborah couldn't hide her pride. "Yes, it did. We have 23 syndicated columns in newspapers, magazines and blogs which bring in good money. When we started, it was just for fun." She flung her head back and said to the ceiling, "But it just kept getting bigger."

"You were both making a tidy sum from this, correct?"

"Much more than we ever expected. We split it 50-50, and we each donate 10% of our share to charity, I give mine to the Children's Hospital in Toronto and Shaye gives," she smacked her own cheek lightly, "I mean she gave hers to St. Jude's Hospital for Children in Los Angeles. I think she went there one time when she was on holiday with her family."

Brampton said nothing and Deb sat quiet looking stunned. Eventually he spoke. "So now you get 100% of the money?"

She looked confused, then angry. "No! We made an agreement that if either of us wanted to stop writing the column the other one would carry on and donate a bigger share of the money to charity. Now it's just me I'll send 25% of the syndication money to her hospital and 25% to mine, and keep the other 50%. You can't blame me for keeping a little more, and Shaye is fine with it," she met Kathy's eyes and didn't correct herself this time. "We always knew one of us would stop before the other, but we never imagined in a million years it would be because one of us," she choked over the last word, "died."

Kathy listened carefully. It was plausible but wildly different to the story she'd been told of the relationship between the two women. She couldn't get her head around it. What about the violent physical encounter at the company party? Everybody had seen that.

"Deb, what about that fight at the company party? Your colleagues say you lashed out at her?"

"Hah! I heard that story, too," Deb spat out. "It's not what happened. Shaye knows tai chi, I'm into martial arts and knife fighting, she does a little karate. We used to spar a bit before we started writing to get the creative juices flowing. We're pretty evenly matched."

Kathy stole a glance at Brampton who was watching Deborah with no expression. She looked back at Deborah and saw a tear roll down her cheek, the first sign of sadness she'd seen from her. It didn't last long. Deb brushed it away roughly and continued.

"What actually happened at the company party was I started to say something about the column. We were having a disagreement about the one we were writing and I wouldn't let it go. We'd vowed not mention it in public, when others were around. So, Shaye went to slap me on the back of the head to shut me up, I moved and got it in the face. I'd just come from training and I guess the adrenaline was flowing. I reared back to give her a kick and pulled it at the last second, but I got her shoulder and she went down. It was a stupid move. So stupid," she laughed unexpectedly, "but it sure took everybody's minds off anything they have overheard!" She was grinning broadly now.

"I think I need a coffee," Kathy said weakly. "Can we take a break? Deb, do you want water or coffee?"

"Water, please," said Deborah and leaned back with her hands behind her head. "Can I get some chips or something, too?"

50. Off The Record

In the corridor, Kathy filled a paper cup at the water fountain while Brampton hit buttons on the vending machine. They peeked through the glass panel on the door and saw Deborah, not so cocky now, staring at the table, looking somehow smaller than when the interview started.

"There's no way she murdered her," Kathy said. "That column was successful because the two of them worked so well together. Where's the benefit to her? What do you think?"

"I agree," he said through a mouthful of chips. "Cross her off the list. We'll go back in there and let her know none of this needs to come out."

Deborah sat up straight as they entered. When they were seated, she leaned across the table with pleading eyes. "So, is that it? Can I go home now? Are you going to expose the Hopkins Sister? It will change things for me at work. A lot of people don't like me and they're going to hold it against me. I might even get fired."

Brampton popped open the second bag of chips for her. "Only three people know your secret and they're all in this room. We can keep it that way."

He turned to speak directly into the recording device. "Computer." A light came on. "Detective Sergeant Sandy Brampton forgot to notify the interviewee this conversation was being recorded. We cannot use Conversation 117488. Please delete it from the system and from the backup system, then turn off the recording."

He paused, his finger on his lips so no one would say anything. "Recording of Detective Sergeant Brampton, Conversation 117488 has been deleted from the system and the backup system. Goodbye," the computer stated and the light went off.

"What about that photograph?" Deborah asked.

Brampton grinned and waved the envelope. "Ain't no photograph."

Deb looked confused. "So how the hell did you find out about this?"

"I asked the lawyer for Shaye's estate to call if he came across anything odd in the will. He found a photograph, a Smith Corona typewriter, a set of golf clubs and other knickknacks left to the Hopkins Sisters that would be picked up within the year by a courier. A note from Shaye would confirm the courier was authentic. Apparently you used the old Smith Corona to write the columns? Part of the Hopkins mystique?"

"That was Shaye's idea," she smiled. "Her grandmother wrote cookbooks and she had a lot of the original recipes done on a janky old typewriter. She loved them and knew it would add to the mystery if we sent original manuscripts done on an old typewriter as well as digital copies."

Brampton was looking very pleased with himself. "I contacted the publisher who said he would send a letter. We kept a watch on the post office box until it was picked up yesterday. Turns out we didn't need to take a picture. My guy recognized you."

He sat up straight and said formally, "Deborah Citlali, we can officially say you are no longer a suspect in the murder of Shaye Alderson."

Deborah straightened, too. "That's it? I'm in the clear? I can go?"

Brampton nodded seriously. Kathy beamed. Deborah stared at them both.

"Well thank you very much, it's been a gas. Kathy you played your part very well. I thought you were genuinely interested in knife fighting, you really worked hard at it."

Kathy looked sheepish. "At first it was just part of the investigation, but I started to get a real rush from it. I learned a lot from you, Deb, not just about the moves. I'm going to keep working out, too, maybe we can work out together?"

Deborah smiled. "Why not? We'll have fun." She stood up and looked questioningly at Brampton who stood, too, and gestured to the door. She did a sudden kick towards him that made him flinch back. She laughed, then held out her hand to him.

"Mr. Brampton, detective, thank you for keeping our secret. But you've gotta find out who killed her. I hope you've got somebody else in mind now I'm in the clear. I loved her, you know. She was a great friend. It was just a charade at work, me the mean bitch and her the nice girl, it kept people guessing. Nobody suspected we had something going together." She sighed. "I'll keep it going as long as I can. I know her style, I can play two roles, and I know she'd want me to, for the charities if nothing else."

She leaned forward, gripping the edge of the table.

"Get the bastard, Mr. Brampton, get him," she hoisted her bag onto her shoulder, "or get her." She turned to the door. "I can go?" He nodded. With her hand on the door-knob she turned back. "When you get them you'd better take good care of them until they're tried, convicted and put away, because if I have my way they won't get that far."

Kathy started to say something, but Deb cut her off. "I know, uttering threats. Silly me." She yanked open the door. "Bite me."

51. Flipping Through Pictures

They sat quietly for a minute after the door slammed. There was one suspect left. They needed to go through those photo albums.

The small boardroom in the station was rarely used and therefore clean and tidy, the chairs were nicely upholstered apart from the coffee stains and Kathy sank into one, glad to be in a different space after hours in interrogation rooms.

Brampton flipped open the lids of the banker's boxes and peered inside. "Anything to tell me before we start going through all these pictures?"

"Grant took most of them seven or eight years ago, and they're mostly around the beach at Channel Lane Point. That alone is interesting, the first murder happened there and Shaye whispered those words to me. There's a lot of landscapes and girls on the beach," she glanced at him, but he responded with a *so what* expression. "The last couple of albums I looked at had pictures of Catrina, it looks like he was infatuated, and a couple are definitely creepy."

Rather than go straight to those photos, Kathy took him through the books in the order she had viewed them. It was slow going. They studied each page searching for clues to the cold case and anything that might connect them to the recent murder.

The light faded outside the windows. Despite its padding, the chair was giving Kathy an ache in her thigh. She got up to pace around the room and did a couple of side kicks to release the tension.

"The martial arts stuff is getting to you," he said drily. She stuck out her tongue. They had never spent such long hours together, a kind of battle-weary companionship had developed.

At last they got to the final albums, she hesitated before digging them out from the box.

"I forgot to say there are some nude photographs here. He was in an artistic phase, exploring the landscape of the body." Brampton raised his eyebrows and she laughed. "Yes, that's what I thought, too, a creative way to pick up liberal-minded girls."

Sure enough, the first page of the second last album featured an unfamiliar girl perched on the arm of a battered armchair in a dorm room. Her demure cross-legged pose was at odds with the white crew cut, ear, nose and lip piercings and a tattoo of Albert Einstein stretching from ankle to knee on one slender leg.

"Moving right along," said Brampton gruffly, flipping the page. Similar photos followed, some better than others, but most poorly lit. The nudes were interspersed with moody shots of snowy courtyards, where nature set the lighting for him. Halfway through, they changed to beach shots and studies of the pretty cottage, straightforward shots, close-ups of woodwork and shingles and studies of the roses round the window.

"Is this the place?"

Kathy nodded. "I think so. Channel Lane Point."

They moved on to the last album which opened with a beach landscape, empty except for a lone young woman staring up at the sky. It was taken with a telephoto lens and Kathy shuddered to think the woman likely thought she was alone.

The next page made Brampton's eyebrows shoot up. Here was the headshot of Catrina Somers, her name in black ink below it. He turned back to the lonely beach figure, was it Catrina? Back to the headshot then on to the next page where he was confronted with the full-length nude. He looked up silently at Kathy who nodded.

It was artful, subtle, carefully posed and undoubtedly Catrina. Brampton flipped through four or five pages of smaller pictures of her, on the beach, walking along a road, some posed, others likely taken with a long lens.

"He was obsessed with her."

Kathy sighed. "I wonder if she ever knew how much he loved her? Maybe he was too shy to tell her, but he couldn't get enough of photographing her."

Brampton leaned in closer and stared hard the next set of photos, the shots taken from outside the cottage through a window framed with roses. Catrina, naked and drying her wet hair, Catrina moving around the room, Catrina seemingly unaware she was being photographed.

Kathy paused for dramatic effect before turning the page, and there she was again, naked in the arms of a fully clothed man. She was bent backwards. The man's face was obscured and so was the hand that held her head, her long hair flowing over it. His other hand was on the small of her back in plain view, but the picture was blurry, the hand looked large but they couldn't make out any detail.

This was potentially the killer, but there was no way to identify him.

They finished the books, making notes here and there but not feeling they'd made any real progress. Kathy pushed her chair back, groaned and waited for him to speak. He rubbed his eyes and said nothing.

"Sandy, we're missing something. I've got this feeling in my belly there's something there. It's not against the law to have photographed a girl who was later murdered, but it's got to mean something. I can't put my finger on it."

Brampton carefully placed the albums back in the boxes and slipped on the lids. "We need to sleep on it. I have to turn my brain off for a bit. Maybe something will come to me in the middle of the night," he stole a glance at her, but she didn't react to the accidental innuendo.

"Let's meet tomorrow at Rosy's and go over it all. We've ruled out a number of people but it won't hurt to revisit everybody and everything, stuff we know for sure and things that still doesn't make sense. We'll get this nailed down."

Little did they know, what they would find would turn the whole case upside down.

52. Digesting Things At Rosy's

Kathy arrived at Rosy's Diner a little after 7:15 in the morning. The day was clear and sunny and she fancifully hoped it might help them see the facts more clearly. She had an idea that she just couldn't put into words yet. Maybe by discussing things with Sandy the blurry images would sharpen and he'd know what to act on.

He arrived moments after she got settled in their usual spot. She watched him walk towards her, thinking how rugged he looked, but so well turned out too. Brown shoes polished to a high shine reflected the intensity with which he approached a case. The gabardine pants had a sharp crease in them that showed his military background. A tan sports coat hung loosely over his shoulders and hit the police issue 45 tucked in the holster under his left arm. She would never call him vain, but he somehow managed to look like he'd stepped out of a GQ magazine ad.

He was looking very cheerful for so early in the morning. She smiled a welcome. "Good morning, Sandy, you look well." She wanted to say *and handsome, too,* but couldn't quite do it.

"Feeling good, Kathy. I'm feeling good. And I'm hungry."

Lucy appeared as if on cue and Kathy wondered, not for the first time, if she could hear everything they said.

Kathy ordered a fruit cup, oatmeal, and hot tea. Sandy was back to bacon and eggs but stopped short of ordering home fries and asked for skim milk with his tea.

"No sugar today, detective?" Lucy was ready to play.

"No need, thank you Lucy, I'm sweet enough." Lucy snorted with delight, Kathy did an eye roll and Lucy nudged her and sauntered away, pocketing her order book.

Brampton grinned at Kathy, who decided it was time to get down to business.

"Right, let's do this. We need to review everything we know so far, see if any puzzle pieces fit together. Let's start with Madeleine now we've heard the full story. If she didn't know about the will the money wasn't a motive, especially now we know she'd worked out a loan with Shaye. She blows hot and cold, sometimes I believe her, other times she seems to be hiding something. What do you think?"

Brampton thought about that. "I'm not crossing anybody off yet, but she's low, very low on the list now. She's got a good reason to act a little shaky or hostile, but she seemed genuine in that interview."

Their breakfasts arrived and for several minutes they concentrated on eating. Kathy put her fork down now and then to jot notes on her pad. Brampton could have easily read them upside down, but he kept his eyes on his bacon. As they filled up, they slowed down and before long they resumed the conversation.

Kathy dabbed delicately at her lips, while Brampton scrubbed at the bacon fat glistening on his. She forced herself to focus. "So if we feel Madeleine is in the clear that brings us to Deborah. I wonder if she's really going to give all that money away to charity." Kathy sipped her coffee and waited for a response. None came. She persisted. "She could double her income from the Hopkins columns, that's a big chunk of change."

"I believe her," he said. "Looks like I believe her more

than you do. There was something genuine about her re-actions, hard to think it might all be fake. The record shows the Hopkins Sisters give away at least 10% of everything to those children's hospitals."

They sat back. That covered the two women. Kathy looked at her notes. "So Grant Ashbury. We've seen from his photos he was obsessed with Catrina at university, and he was infatuated with Shaye at high school, then years later when she turns up at work. Pretty strange co-incidence to have strong feelings for two dead women, but it's hard to think of him killing them. If the dagger is instrumental, he's not a Stormont man and so not really part of the ceremony." She couldn't believe she was giving consideration to the twisted, misogynist family ritual. She stopped talking, stared at the table, then her head snapped up.

"I thought about those photographs all night and I've got an idea. We need to get back and look at them right now!" She pushed her plate away. As if by magic, Lucy appeared with their bills. They had a hard and fast rule that each paid for their own meal.

"You're amazing Lucy, how do you always know when we want the bill? Sometimes before we do?" Kathy asked as she gathered her things.

"Trade secrets my friend," said the perky woman tapping the side of her nose. "I can't reveal them or I'll be barred from the grand waitress club of old-time diners."

Kathy laughed. She loved the routine with Lucy.

53. Look Real Close

Back at Brampton's office Kathy went straight for the album she'd been thinking about, yanked it from the banker's box and flipped pages recklessly until she found the one she was after. She slowed down and pulled it carefully from its sleeve.

"Can you scan this? Preview it on the screen first so I can tell you the exact area to focus on."

Brampton raised his eyebrows and watched her pacing. He quite liked it when she told him what to do. He wondered was that a bad thing? He slipped the photo onto the scanning bed and waited until it appeared on his screen. Kathy leaned in close and peered at the picture. He stepped back, but not very far, and leaned over her shoulder to look. It was Catrina on the beach with a man with long sun-bleached hair. It was one of the pictures Grant had taken with a telephoto lens. The man was in profile, but his face was not clear.

"Can you close in on their heads please and drop it into Photoshop."

Brampton did as he was told and the two heads appeared on the screen. Kathy took the mouse and roughly outlined the long fair hair, cutting it short. She added a moustache and full beard. Then she coloured it all black. Brampton watched and his eyes widened.

"Son of a bitch!"

It was a quick, rough job, but they both saw it. Kathy turned to him, surprised he was so close. She didn't pull back but looked up into his eyes and he said what she was thinking. "That's a young Ken Rivers!"

"Oh my God, Sandy, where's the other picture? The one with the man holding her in the cottage."

He flipped the pages in the album she'd pulled out, didn't find what he was looking for, went back to the banker's box and lifted the album they had examined last. He laid it open on his desk and flipped pages. There it was. Another shot taken with a long lens, through the window of the Channel Lane Point cottage. He scanned it. They stared at it for a moment.

Kathy grabbed the mouse and traced around Shaye's head and shoulders, blew it up and enhanced it, filling in pixels to give a solid picture.

"The hand on her neck, it's blurred but it looks too big. Could that be a deerskin glove? Bloody hell, could this be the moment she was stabbed?"

Brampton saved the cropped image then reverted to the full-length shot. The person holding her had shoulder-length, sun bleached hair. *Bleached being the operative word,* he thought.

"We need to talk to Ken Rivers," Kathy was saying. "But we've shared so much with him, I don't want to spook him. Let me phone and see if he's at the University. I can ask to drop by and see him tonight."

She took out her phone and dialled his number. She listened to it ring and eventually got the message that he wasn't in, please leave your name, number and a brief message.

Her message was short and, she hoped, casual. "Hey Ken, it's Kathy. I have another question about the history of the dagger. Can I drop round tomorrow morning, perhaps you can help me understand some things? It's Kathy

Chatsworth," she said again and grimaced at Brampton. He made a dismissive gesture and mouthed, *it's okay.* She took a breath. "Umm, it's Wednesday and the time is 10:56 a.m. Byee!"

Brampton was frowning. "Maybe I should go with you."

"Nope," she said firmly. "Thank you, but it's better if I go alone. I'll find out a lot more. He thinks I'm just interested, he knows you're a cop."

He looked hard at her, then nodded and turned back to the banker's box. "Let's go through the stuff we looked at yesterday. We might see more of good old Ken now we know he was there."

For the next 40 minutes they leafed through albums. The fair-haired man could be seen in pictures of Catrina, sometimes barely in the frame, sometimes in the distance, sometimes close, never a full shot of his face. Both were now sure it was Rivers with a blond, shoulder-length do.

"He had a thing with Catrina. We know he was involved with Shaye, Madeline said they were flirting at the Stormont mansion. Oh Sandy, he could be our guy. But he's smart. If he thinks we're onto him ..."

He threw caution to the wind. He grabbed her arms, looked hard into her eyes. "You can go, but be careful. I can be right outside." She shook her head, and he shook her gently. "You're not doing this alone."

***

Using speed dial Brampton called Kathy. He'd had a call from a panicked Gordon Stormont and when she picked up he got straight to the point.

"Just had a call from Gordon. The dagger and gloves are missing from the box. He's only just had them returned to him. Did you find Ken?"

"He's not at the University, but I think I know where he is. He disappeared yesterday and nobody has heard from him. He missed his morning class and he's never missed one before, ever. I take it the gloves and dagger went missing early this morning?

"They were there last night. Get this, Gordon said Ken came by last, he was agitated. He asked to see the dagger, they talked about what's happened, they shared a glass of Scotch but then Rivers left in a hurry."

"I think I know where he is," said Kathy. "I'm going there now. You'd better come too. Give me a head start, but hang back. I'll talk to him. Wait for my call."

She explained to him where she thought Dr. Ken Rivers would be and why. She was sure he had the dagger and gloves. She was sure he wouldn't hurt her. Before Brampton could object she hung up and ran to her car.

She punched an address into the GPS, the journey time was half an hour. She was going to Channel Lane Point.

54. Confronting A Killer

Kathy turned off the highway onto a narrow, tree-lined road that led to Channel Lane Point and the cottage. She thought carefully about how to approach Rivers. She was not going to be the next victim.

About half a mile along the winding road she spotted his car and pulled up beside it. It was still a hundred yards from the cottage. There was a clearing off to the left with a rustic, carved bench in the centre. The sun bathed the old bench with light. She quietly got out of the car clutching her phone. She looked left and right, not really expecting to see anyone but her self-preservation instinct was on high alert. She moved quietly. She didn't want to startle Ken Rivers.

As she walked, she thought it was a good idea to have her hands free so she could defend herself if Ken tried anything. She tucked the phone in her front pants pocket.

The bench was thick and heavy with deep carving on the back. It was positioned to catch the late afternoon sun. Someone was sitting there, bent forward, head in his hands. It was Dr. Kent Rivers.

Kathy stopped and speed dialled Brampton. Voicemail. Her heart sank. She spoke quickly and softly. "He's here at the Channel Point Lane cottage. He's sitting in a clearing before you get to the house. You'll see our cars. He's alone, but you'd better bring backup. No sirens. I'm going to talk to him." She disconnected, straightened her shoulders and walked calmly to the bench, stopping a few feet away.

"Hello Ken."

The man started and turned around. His eyes were wide, like a startled animal, then they drooped and his face fell. He looked tired, weary and haunted.

"Kathy Chatsworth. I thought you might come," the words rattled from his throat. Then he smiled. "Kathy. Of course you are here. You are the Blessed One. You can take this curse from me." He began to rise, but she motioned him to sit back down and walked slowly to the bench. She perched at the opposite end.

"Ken. Do you want to talk about it?" She was keeping her voice steady, trying to sound encouraging, trying to sound unafraid. She saw him thinking about what to say. He reached out his hand to her, but stopped and put it down on the bench between them. He was wearing the deerskin gloves. It took all she had to not pull back, to not move her hand away.

He sighed. "It's true. I am cursed. And it's all come unravelled. I am a slave to my fate, but you, Kathy Chatsworth, you held my beautiful Shaye as she died. You are blessed. You are here because you are the one true love."

This was unexpected.

Kathy fought down her panic. She watched his chest swell as he pulled in a breath, then sink as he let it out in a long weary sigh. He pulled back his gloved hand. He had the dagger in his right hand and laid the blade deliberately across his left hand. She recognized the movement. The ceremony was unfolding. A chill coursed through her veins and she tensed, ready to defend herself, but he remained slumped, unmoving, staring into the distance.

"I really thought Shaye was the one to help me continue the blood line," he turned to her, his eyes narrowed. "As the mystery cousin I *am* part of the bloodline you know." He patted the seat of the heavy oak bench. "And this, this is a Stormont bench. I had it made and put here. There's a crest on the back.

What was he talking about? This was news. She raised her eyebrows, said nothing. She forced her face to show nothing, she hid her curiosity. She just nodded. He needed to talk at his own pace – and he did.

"My father," he was staring at her now. "My father was the bastard son of Clive Benson Stormont. Clive Stormont supported my grandmother and the child, but he never acknowledged us. He never acknowledged us, but my father was a Stormont," he was shouting now. "I am a Stormont!" He raised the dagger and Kathy drew back, but the blade fell back onto the open palm of his left hand and he said softly, a sob in his voice. "I am a Stormont, and I am part of the legend, and I am cursed."

55. Kathy's Training Pays Off

Kathy exhaled long and slow. Quietly she said, "Oh Ken. Ken. Tell me about Shaye."

He snapped his head up and glared. She gazed evenly back, and his face relaxed. "I told her I had something important to ask. I had to see her. I went to her house. When I walked in she had her back to me. She turned around and saw I was holding the dagger and was wearing the gloves and ... and she laughed. She laughed at me. She said I was a fool and she could never love me. She walked over and sat down on that wretched couch. I should have just left, but I was too excited. I had rehearsed the words, and I was passionate, and I couldn't stop myself." He closed his eyes.

Kathy watched his face. He was reliving the moment, his eyes moved behind closed lids.

"I couldn't stop myself," he repeated. "I started to say the words, but she was smirking, she stood up and knocked the dagger out of my hand. She laughed at me again."

He paused, looking off into the distance, taking himself back to the pretty little house.

"She disgraced the dagger," he said coldly. "She knocked it to the floor. She should have taken it in her hand. I picked it up and I knew she had to die. I stabbed her in the right place," he said, his eyes on hers, an odd expression on his face, pride mixed with despair. "I did it correctly. But when I withdrew the dagger, I wasn't holding her properly, she was still moving, damn her. She lunged to the side, she tripped on the coffee table, she fell down and smashed her face." He sobbed. "Her beautiful face."

His grip on the dagger's hilt tightened, Kathy was prepared to spring off the bench if he made a move, but he went on talking.

"I knew then I was cursed. I had failed. Failed! I didn't hold her properly. I didn't lay her down as the ceremony demands. Like my unhappy ancestor 300 years ago, I was cursed forever. I panicked and fled."

He turned to look at her again, and she raised her eyes from the blade to his face.

"The curse started right there," he said bitterly. "I ran away, down the path, but as I went through that damned hedge the dagger caught on the gatepost. It flew out of my hand. I didn't see where it landed. I couldn't see it but I had to get away. I was in a panic, I ran back to my car and drove away. I don't know how I didn't crash the car. I, I, was shattered. Shaye was dead. She refused me. But all I could think of was how I had failed in the ritual and now the curse would follow me all of my life."

He was out of breath. He was very still. Then he raised his head and looked at her. His expression made her blood run cold. "And now there's you. You are blessed. You are flowing over with good luck, you have the magic, Kathy. You found the dagger that was lost, you held the maiden as she died, you walked right into the legend."

He got to his feet, she drew back in alarm. He stood looking at her, though he didn't seem to be focusing. "Now you will be my true love and you will take this curse away."

Kathy sat perfectly still as Rivers started to say the

ritual words. He spoke in a monotone, swaying slightly, holding the dagger out to her. "You are the pure one, the blessed one. Kathy Chatsworth you are my one true love, will you ..." He moved toward her and the weeks of fight training came back in a rush. Her left foot flew out catching his right wrist and knocked the dagger from his hand. She followed up with her right foot, catching him in the back of the knees and knocked him to the ground. She stood over him, her foot raised to strike again, but he stayed down, clutching his knee and moaning.

"Why did you do that?" His voice was a whine. "Ouch, Kathy, ouch. I wasn't going to stab you. Kathy, you're the lady in the legend, the one who will save me, who will take the curse off me. I just want to ask you to marry me, and you're going to say yes."

Kathy moved over to him and saw his trance was broken. He was in pain. She reached out, he took her hand and she pulled him up. He sat heavily on the bench, rubbing his wirst then his leg. He looked stricken and very old as he turned his face to hers. A tear ran down his cheek.

"Maybe I was already cursed," he said. "Maybe it all started with Catrina."

Kathy held her breath. When he didn't continue, she said softly, "Did you get the ceremony right with Catrina?"

56. Cold Case Closed

He smiled slyly. "I wondered if you would understand about the ladies who went before. Catrina was special. I let her stay in my cottage rent-free. She was like a child of nature, she loved to be naked and free. So beautiful. We were in love." He said it defiantly, as if he was trying to convince himself.

His eyes closed as he took himself back to the moment. When he opened them, they were clear and bright. "Catrina knew all about the ceremony. She knew the words, and when I started to say them she was fascinated, transfixed. She stood there in all her beauty. I handed her the dagger and she smiled and took it. She knew what it meant, she knew how I felt. She should have known what she was doing. Catrina *committed herself* to death. She'd studied the ceremony, it was part of the paper she was writing with the others." He sounded petulant now. He stopped talking. The silence stretched until Kathy thought he was not going to finish his confession, but just as she was about to speak, he shook himself and carried on.

"She handed it back." He spat out the words. "She handed back the dagger. She said she didn't love me and that she could never marry me. She touched my cheek and turned away, but I stepped up beside her and put my gloved hand behind her neck. She looked me in the eyes and said, 'you're going to kill me because of a legend?' I told her the legend demands it, she knew that." He rubbed his leg again, rested his hands on his knees and said calmly, "Catrina knew what would happen if she rejected me. She knew she would die. At first she struggled, but then she grew calm and resigned to her fate."

Kathy felt a flush of anger and fought down a sharp reply. She hoped Sandy would arrive soon. Her fear was fading but her contempt for Dr. Ken Rivers was growing. Luckily, he was oblivious.

"I stabbed her quickly and held her as she fell. I held her until she passed to a better place." He seemed to be savouring the memory, the confession, the re-telling of what he thought of as a glorious ritual. To him it was his birthright, not a brutal murder.

"After she passed, I washed her body. I picked her up and put her on the bed and covered her. She was so peaceful, so beautiful." He sighed.

There was no point talking to him about the murder, because to him it was not murder. Unless he was a very good actor, he honestly believed he was following his fate, honouring his heritage, playing his part in a bizarre ceremony that had been followed for hundreds of years.

As they sat silently, she wondered what was going through his mind but decided not to ask. She would retrieve the dagger instead.

"I'm going to go and find the dagger," she said gently. "It needs to be returned to Gordon Stormont. When I find it, do you want to hold it until the others come?"

"The others?" He looked bewildered. "Oh the police. Yes please. Yes, I would like that very much," he shivered. "I hope they come soon, I'm growing cold."

Kathy searched the area where she'd seen the dagger fly. It took her a few moments but, once again, the sun found the green stone as if to draw her to it. Maybe she *was* part of the legend. She picked up the ornamental dagger and carried it with two hands back to Rivers. She handed it to him handle first and he cradled it in his lap.

She had recorded their entire conversation on her iPhone tucked in her pants pocket. But she had the feeling Dr. Ken Rivers was going to repeat the story to anyone who would listen. He seemed proud of what he had accomplished, proud of his devotion to the legend, unconcerned about the death of two women.

As Kathy was handing him the dagger, Brampton and four police offers came over the ridge of the hill. He broke into a run when he saw her with the knife, but she looked up and waved, and he relaxed. He holstered his gun but the others remained on alert, weapons pointed at the man sitting on the big Stormont bench.

Brampton put his arm around her shoulders and she moved into his hug. He held her tight and she turned her face to his, but instead of the kiss he had suddenly and wildly hoped for, she put her lips to his ear and said, "He confessed to killing Catrina Somers and Shaye Anderson. I have it recorded on my iPhone. Let me take the dagger back from him and the gloves. I think he'll let me. If you or your people try, he might turn ugly. He truly believes I can save him from the curse."

He held her tighter, then pulled away. "Good work, Kathy," he whispered and let her go, slowly drawing his gun from its holster and holding it beside his leg.

Kathy moved closer to Rivers, who was sitting with his head tipped to the sun, eyes closed, ignoring the police. "My friend, I need the dagger and the gloves so I can give them back to Gordon Stormont. They'll be needed for the next ceremony."

He opened his eyes and looked at her sadly, then raised

the dagger between them and, holding the blade, offered her the green bejewelled handle. She took it in her right hand and cradled the blade on her left arm, performing the ceremony as he would expect. He took off the deer gloves and handed them to her, then buried his face in his hands, like a tortured soul. "What have I done? What have I done to those wonderful women?"

Kathy wrapped the gloves around the wicked blade and handed them to Brampton. She knew the story was far from over. The legend of the dagger would live on. How many other women would have their palms gently pricked or their hearts cruelly stopped by this terrible thing? She hoped Gordon Stormont would put an end to the ridiculous bloody legend. His son was just 11 years old. Would they risk ending the tradition? Remembering Gordon's childlike enthusiasm for family stories, she rather doubted it.

Epilogue

When Kathy arrived at the diner Brampton was in their usual booth and his sombre face broke into a smile when he saw her. She slid into the opposite seat and reached across to squeeze his hand briefly before picking up the menu. Neither spoke.

Lucy approached and saw them sitting in silence. She'd read the report in the newspaper about the arrest of Dr. Rivers for the murders of two women, and she'd been expecting them for their post-review meeting. She took their orders quickly without the usual banter and turned away.

"How did it go with Rivers at the police station," Kathy said at last.

He snorted. "He was a pompous ass. He spent some time being the professor taking us through just how well he'd performed the ceremony when he killed Catrina. He talked a lot about the curse and finally got around to what happened with Shaye. He still believes if he finds the right girl, he'll marry her and they'll be part of the legend and everything will be all right. Pompous, and delusional, too."

When Lucy appeared with their coffee, he stopped abruptly. Kathy glanced up and said softly, "Thanks Lucy," and the waitress withdrew.

Brampton dumped in two heaped spoonfuls of sugar, stirred and sipped. "He even talked about changing his name to Rivers-Stormont. I suppose he figures he's earned legitimacy now and has the right to wear the name. He said history students in the future will come to see the tragedy and triumph of his part in the Stormont Dagger legacy. I'm not sure he'll ever go to trial. He's been taken to the psych ward, and it might be some time before he admits to himself these were murders of innocent women, not some inevitable chapter in some damned story or a step on the road to claiming his twisted heritage."

Kathy put her elbows on the table and her chin in her hands and looked at him. "Shhhh," she said and reached across to hold his hand. He felt his shoulders relax.

"Sandy, I talked to Madeline yesterday. She was upset but glad we found out who killed Shaye. Her husband is doing much better with the new therapy and she's hopeful he will walk soon. As for the lawsuit, Jackson Junior at the law firm got her husband's company to provide an unusually large settlement. I guess they didn't want the PR nightmare of refusing to compensate a decorated war vet whose wife lost her sister to a deluded academic." She smiled wryly. "Not while it's fresh in the papers anyway."

Brampton grunted in agreement. "Are you still training with Deborah?"

"Absolutely. It saved my life in the Ken situation, and you never know what's lurking round the corner. Deb and I have become good friends," she said. "We meet up regularly for tea or a drink, I enjoy her company."

Lucy arrived with their breakfasts, put them down and quietly walked away, she was burning with curiosity, but relieved to see them chatting more cheerfully.

"Grant called me yesterday," Kathy said, munching on her bacon. With the case solved, and feeling happy to be alive and well, she was indulging herself with eggs, bacon, mushrooms and home fries, plus some healthy blueberries on the side. "He thanked me for our work, for finding out what happened to the two women he loved. We talked about a few other things, and I found out he's seeing a young lady who used to be his assistant. She's moved to another firm so they're free to date. I hope he finds true love, poor Grant, he really is a nice guy, like everybody says. He deserves it." She sipped her coffee and sat back contentedly.

Brampton shrugged. "He's had some rough luck. I hope he doesn't worry too much about the possible fate of this latest love."

Kathy looked horrified, then laughed. "Third time lucky?" she said, feeling guilty then gratified when he chuckled.

He watched her with affection, wondering what their next case would be. On the one hand he couldn't hope for another crime to be committed just so he could spend more time with Kathy Chatsworth. On the other hand he knew it was inevitable. And he couldn't help feeling glad.

Pistols in the Park

By
Janet Davies
And
Stephen Rayfield

Kathy Chatsworth Mystery 2

Chapter 1 Guns in the Mist

Kathy Chatsworth was enjoying a power walk in the park. It was a cool September morning with mist rising from cold wet grass and a dazzling sun breaking free of the trees, and she was feeling a little natural high on the smell of autumn leaves when she heard the gunshot.

She spun round to the east, looking straight into the sun and, shading her eyes, she saw a figure at the top of the hill. Then she heard another noise, the sound of human wailing, and broke into a run up the hill.

When she reached the top, she found a man on the ground with a hole in his chest oozing red blood into the green grass. As she knelt and felt for a pulse, she heard a whimper and whirled round to see a woman collapsing on the ground, with a gun in her hand. She glanced quickly back to the bloody man then, finding no trace of a heartbeat, turned to the woman.

Kathy knelt and wrapped the bottom of her t-shirt around the woman's trembling hand and prised the gun from her fingers. The woman was pale, sobbing and shaking as Kathy pulled her into her arms. The face was wet with tears, her eyes wild, but the voice was soft. "I should have shot him again!" she hissed, then fainted.

Kathy fumbled for her phone and hit speed dial. She didn't call 911, she called Detective Sandy Brampton, figuring he would be handed the case, so why go through a middleman? He picked up after two rings.

"Brampton, how can I help you, Kathy?"

"I've got another one," she almost shouted, then added more quietly, "In Midland Park. I'm up on Pridmore hill sitting beside a dead man, and there's a lady in my lap with a gun in her hand." Sandy waited. "I'm pretty sure he's dead, but you'd better bring an ambulance for the woman." She paused, "I took away the gun." She waited for his response.

Brampton's first thought was, *"How does she do it? This is a quiet town, but she runs across a lot of stiffs."* But that wasn't fair. She had discovered one other corpse in the time he'd known her, but she'd got herself involved in the investigation of a lot more crimes. His second thought was *she's touched the gun and compromised the crime scene. Dr. MacDugon is not going to be pleased.*

Up on the hill, Kathy checked again for a pulse and decided the man really was gone. He was a nice-looking guy, apart from the ruined chest. The woman in her lap was breathing steadily but she was out cold, the gun resting on her chest where Kathy had carefully placed it. She studied it. She was no expert but she could see it was a small one, a lady's gun, maybe what they called a *Saturday night special.* She frowned. She didn't like that expression much, it was callous and smart-ass, like calling a muscle t-shirt a *wife beater.*

She took a deep breath. *Yoga breathing,* she thought, *be calm.* But she was worried a jogger or dog-walker might appear and ask questions or trample on the evidence.

She tried to recall the last time she'd seen Detective Sergeant Brampton. Kathy Chatsworth was a journalist. The press and police are not usually known for their warm relationships, but she and Sandy worked well together. He thought she was over-enthusiastic to the point of fool-hardiness sometimes, but she occasionally found him infuriating, too. She smiled at the thought.

Brampton was smart, but cautious. She respected his clear thinking and discipline, but they could drive her a little nuts when her instinct was to break through rules and regulations and paperwork and just solve a crime.

The woman in her lap groaned and Kathy's heart leapt, but she showed no signs of waking up.

She thought back to their last collaboration on a case she had labelled in her files *A Dagger for Danger.* Despite some dreadful circumstances, she gave whimsical titles to cases she got involved with, whether covering for the newspaper or assisting her detective friend.

As a student, she'd dreamed of writing novels, but working on high school newspapers revealed a flair for investigative reporting. After university she gravitated to the daily press and now had a weekly column, which gave her ample time to moonlight with Sandy Brampton.

The dagger murder case had been awful. Innocent women had been slaughtered, there were several suspects, but her insight and his dogged determination led them to the killer.

But that was then. Right now, Kathy's ass was damp, sitting on wet grass with two inert bodies for company and a chill creeping through her blue track pants. She was relieved when Brampton walked up the hill. Her heart sank a little when she recognized the district coroner Dr. Linda MacDugon right behind him.

MacDugon immediately knelt by the victim. After a few moments she rose.

"Well, you've found me another hot body, Kathy."

"Yes ma'am, and I'm learning the ropes. Other than checking for a pulse I didn't do *anything* to screw up the crime scene. I used my t-shirt to move the gun."

"So that person laying on top of you is not part of the crime scene? It looks like you've touched *her* plenty. We're goanna need your clothes."

Kathy groaned. She'd been careful not to touch the gun, but of course fibres from her t-shirt would be on it, and the comatose woman would be transferring forensic evidence, maybe even gunpower residue, to Kathy's clothes, to the ground and God knows what else. She was undeniably part of the crime scene herself now, but there was no way she could have kept her distance, was there?

Fortunately, she wore a sturdy sports bra and decent underpants, but she wasn't thrilled about stripping off in front of them. Brampton was taking off his jacket to give her when the coroner pulled a pair of grey coveralls from her bag and thrust them at Kathy.

"Here you go." She turned her back and pulled Brampton around with her. "He's dead. Multiple gunshot wounds centered round the heart. First shot probably killed him, the others were likely just emotion but we'll know more after I get him back to the office."

The unconscious woman stirred in Kathy's lap. *Thank God, my legs are getting numb,* Kathy thought. The woman didn't try to rise, just stared blankly at them and flinched as Brampton knelt down.

"Stay calm, ma'am. I'm taking the gun. We'll get you out of here as soon as we can." He took a wooden chopstick from his breast pocket and slipped it through the handle of the gun, then dropped it into an evidence bag and sealed it.

He stood up and Linda MacDugon took his place. "Miss, I need to bag your hands, and I'll need your sweater. When we get to the police station, I'll have your shirt and pants, too, but we'll give you something to wear."

The woman submitted meekly. Colour was returning to her cheeks and Kathy noted she was young. Linda turned to Kathy. "Your turn. You didn't touch the gun, but let's do it right, so some smart DA doesn't jump all over it in the future."

Kathy gently removed the woman from her lap and sat her up, then stood up herself. Her feet were numb. She hobbled over to Linda and held out her hands to be swabbed.

Paramedics had arrived with a gurney. They checked one more time to confirm they really did have a dead man then turned to the live young woman who now seemed fully recovered and was insisting she could walk by herself. But procedures had to be followed. Before climbing onto the gurney, she turned to Sandy and said, "Please, can I kick him? Just once?"

Brampton kept a straight face. "No ma'am, we'll just leave him be for now."

She nodded seriously, climbed onto the gurney and laid back with her arms folded over her chest.

...

The sun rose higher and Kathy stood gratefully in its warmth wearing the spare coverall. She was glad they hadn't taken her underwear.

Crime scene tape was wrapped around the brow of the hill and officers stood guard, giving curt answers to the curious joggers and dog walkers who gathered.

"Okay, now tell me what you know about the scene," Sandy said, and she carefully went through all that had happened from the sound of the gunshot to his arrival. She was still shivering slightly, and he resisted the urge to put his arms around her, just nodded gravely and took notes.

"When I saw the woman, she didn't look dangerous, she had slumped to the ground, so I just took the gun from her and got hold of her and then she passed out." Kathy had been staring into the distance, but now she turned to him, looked around to see if anyone was close enough to hear, then leaned in and said quietly, "Get this. Before she fainted, she said, *'I should have shot him again.'* A pretty damning thing to say, right?"

He closed his notebook and placed his hand on her shoulder. *Here we go,* he thought. "Maybe. But things aren't always what they seem. My job would be so much easier if they were. I'm going with her in the ambulance. Wanna come?"

Kathy glanced down at the grey jumpsuit. It was wide enough for two people but short in the leg, showing three inches of bare shin between the elasticated ankle and her sports socks. She placed her bagged hand over his and looked into his eyes. "Absolutely, there's a murder to solve here."

The woman was now fully conscious and didn't seem hostile. Sandy would try to get some information from her before they got to the station. Who was she, why did she have a gun, who was the man and why did she want to kick his corpse again?

About Janet Davies and Stephen Rayfield

Jan Davies and Stephen Rayfield collaborate on the engaging Kathy Chatsworth Mysteries, he plots the stories while she brings the interesting characters to life or death.

It started as a love for writing and reading murder mysteries. Now it has blossomed into the world of Kathy Chatsworth and Sandy Brampton.

If you like reading a good old fashion murder mystery who done it with clever twists and turns to keep you questioning who is the real murderer, we hope you enjoyed this first book in the series.

We sincerely thank all those who leave reviews - they really help share with others Kathy Chatsworth mysteries.

Enjoy your murder mystery reading!

Janet Davies and Stephen Rayfield